IN THE NIGHT!

Charley jumped when the noise of a gun blast tore open the night. The approaching man jerked and gasped, and pitched forward as if he had been struck from behind with a club. Blood stained the back of his leather jacket, spreading out slowly to drip from his body into the snow. Charley watched with intense shock, and Bo cursed.

Charley rushed into the street and on past the prone outlaw. He knew he was dead even without checking, for the shot had struck him in the center of his body, knocking him sprawling and no doubt tearing up his insides. Charley was not particularly concerned, but he wanted whoever fired that shot. Whoever it was, he had knocked out Dry Creek's only chance at gaining an advantage over the Murphy gang. . . .

Other *Leisure* books by Cameron Judd:

BEGGAR'S GULCH
CORRIGAN
THE TREASURE OF JERICHO MOUNTAIN

BAD NIGHT
AT DRY CREEK

CAMERON JUDD

LEISURE BOOKS NEW YORK CITY

LEISURE BOOKS ®

December 2004

Dorchester Publishing Co., Inc.
200 Madison Avenue
New York, NY 10016

ISBN 0-8439-5286-5

The name "Leisure Books" and the stylized "L" with design are
trademarks of Dorchester Publishing Co., Inc.

Printed in the United States of America.

Visit us on the web at www.dorchesterpub.com.

Chapter 1

Charley Hanna shivered in the chill Colorado wind, but he refused to return to the house. Instead he paced about the yard, smoking, casting occasional glances over his shoulder toward the door, watching the wispy smoke rising black against the gray of the sky from the chimney. He would have liked to sit by that fire where it was warm, but the old lady had never liked him to smoke indoors, and with the doctor there and the threat of death hanging so heavy inside those walls it was a heck of a lot more comfortable outside, even with the cold. At least a man could smoke.

He looked once more at the house and wondered if the old lady was all right. He tossed his cigarette into the dirty snow and listened to the faint sizzling sound it made as he dug into his vest pocket for his tobacco pouch.

"The old lady," he muttered to himself, giving a sort of snort to punctuate the title. What way was that for a man to talk about his own mother? She deserved more respect than that. The old lady indeed!

But that was how his father had always referred to her, and there had been no lack of love on his part. And Charley loved her too, and worried about her now that she was ailing. Good thing his Pa was dead, he thought. He wouldn't have been able to stand seeing Ma laid up and sick. Pa was like that. He had been a powerful strong lawman all his days, but when it came to Ma he was as weak as mush. Strong men were like that, Charley mused. Look inflinching down the muzzle of a rifle and then wilt when it came to women. Pa had been that way, and Charley was just like him.

Everyone thought Charley was just like his pa in almost every way. After all, he had taken over the same job, working as town marshal here in Dry Creek, walking with the same slump, wearing the same old pistol, cussing at the same old dog at the jailhouse doorstep—a dog that had been ancient when Charley was a youth, but somehow just flat refused to die.

It had been hard when Pa died, but Charley had made it all right. In a way he hadn't felt too bad, for Pa had died peaceful on his bed, dying in a natural way, not choking out his life with a chest full of slugs like it might have been. Things were more civilized now than they had been in Pa's days, Charley knew, but still there was a rough edge to living that might not wear off for years to come.

Ma. How was she? What was taking that fool doctor so long? It was hard to believe she was sick; it had always seemed to Charley she would live forever. At least that was how it should be. But it had been two months since she had been out of bed, and every day she looked a bit weaker. And then last night something had happened—Charley didn't know just what, but he knew it was bad—and now the doc had been in there the longest time, and Charley half longed and half dreaded to see him come out.

Another cigarette fizzled out in the snow. Charley kicked up a piece of snow and frozen turf, then glanced once more toward the door. He paused, frowned, then moved toward it. And at the base of the steps he stopped again and cursed. The thought crossed his mind that praying might be more the thing to do than cursing.

But he was poor at the former and good at the latter, so what was the use of trying? And if old Doc Hopkins couldn't save Ma, it didn't seem likely that even the Good Lord could. That was the way it seemed to Charley, at least. He knew he wasn't religious enough—Ma had told him that many times, and she was always right—but he had quit worrying about it long ago. He had tried religion, and tried it hard, but it had never stuck with him. It seemed it just wouldn't take, somehow.

The door opened and Charley's newest cigarette, not even yet crimped shut, dropped from his fingers. It was Katherine at the door.

"Kathy—is the doc. . ."

Old Doc Hopkins came out of the door behind Kathy, pulling on his worn overcoat. He had always worn that same overcoat, as long as Charley could remember. He didn't even give Charley a chance to ask how Ma was.

"Charley, I've always been straight with all my patients and their families, and I won't change now. Your ma's in a bad way, and I don't think we can be too optimistic. Course you can't never tell."

"What's the matter with her, Doc?"

"Blood clot hit her brain, paralyzed her left side. Must have happened in the night sometime. It's nothin' unusual. It's the same thing that killed your Pa."

Charley opened his mouth to speak, then realized suddenly there was really nothing to say. Doc Hopkins coughed and it sent out a white cloud of steam from his lips. Charley watched it fade away, then dropped his gaze to his boot.

"Can you say how long she has, Doctor?" Kathy asked in a slightly choked voice.

The old man grunted. "Only the Lord can say, girl. That's beyond anything an old country doctor can predict."

7

There came a silence then, and when Charley realized there was nothing else to be said, he thanked the doctor and moved up on the porch beside Kathy. The old doctor wheezed out to his buggy, coughing loudly, his shoulders stooped. It took him a long time and a lot of effort to crawl up into the driver's seat. He clicked his tongue and jerked the lines, and the buggy clattered off on the frozen gravel of the road.

"His cough is bad. I wouldn't be surprised if it was consumption," Kathy said.

Charley said nothing, but turned and entered the house. Kathy looked after him for a long time, and in her eyes was something unreadable.

Sarah Redding pulled her shawl a little closer around her and stared out the window. The sky had a gray look to it, cold and threatening. So far the snows had been small, but it wouldn't be long until the first heavy snow blanketed the Rockies and the Dry Creek community. She was grateful for the warmth of the cabin and the huge stock of firewood outside. She had prepared well for the winter, carefully re-chinking the cracks in the wall, laying in supplies for months ahead. When the snows came she would be ready.

She looked around the cabin. It was lonesome, somehow, but she tried to ignore the feeling. She had learned over the years to shove it aside, to lose it in the bustle of everyday business. It helped her to forget the emptiness that had eaten away at her since John died.

John. . .what a husband he had been, working hard, building a secure home for her, talking in anticipation of the family they would raise together. It had filled her soul with joy and a longing for the future. When he had died, killed in such an absurd manner, crushed beneath a tree that was to provide winter fuel, she had almost yielded up hope. But there was no choice but to live and do the best she could, to continue the dream that had been so swiftly destroyed. She hoped many times on her bed at night that John was proud of her.

The farm seemed empty now without a man's hand at work on it. But she had a fierce pride in all she had accomplished and was determined she would make it. Still, sometimes it was so lonely. . . .

Her attention was drawn suddenly to a stirring on down the road, a movement where the bend curved around the trees. A rider was approaching, slowly, his horse's breath sending out regular double puffs of white mist. She felt her skin crawling. There were few riders out this way; who could it be?

Her heart leaped suddenly in anticipation. Charley Hanna! Maybe he was coming to see her. . .she couldn't be sure yet if it was him, but it looked like his horse. Her breath quickened and a smile played at her lips. Charley Hanna was the only man since John had died who could make her heart beat faster. Her hands fumbled at the knot of her apron, and she wondered where she had laid her comb.

She glanced again out the window, and her heart fell. It wasn't Charley. This was a stranger. She eyed him with suspicion. Why was he riding all the way out here to this remote farm? She looked at him closely, trying to draw up recognition from her memory. It was no use. He was unknown to her.

Into the yard he rode, but he did not dismount. She peered around the curtain and frowned.

She stepped back into the center of the cabin, unnerved. The stranger didn't call, nor dismount. Instead he was staring at the cabin, silent, and that bothered her. Hesitating, she reached above the cabinet against the wall and removed a small derringer. Quickly she checked it. It was loaded.

She moved over to the door. Still no sound from

outside, only the faint whinny of the horse. She reached out to the latch, then withdrew her hand. Biting her lip, she frowned. Her hand felt cold against the bone handle of the derringer.

He called out then, softly. Strange. . .something in his voice was wrong. She moved over to the window again. He was very pale, and trembling, and apparently not only from the cold.

A low cry emerged from her throat as she saw him slump slowly over the saddlehorn, then slide limply to the earth. One foot still hung in the stirrup; his horse stepped restlessly. She noticed a stain of red on his side.

Without hesitation she threw open the door. The cold air struck her suddenly, chilling her body through the thin fabric of her dress. She ran over to his side, hesitated uncertainly, then loosened his boot heel from the stirrup. His leg fell like lead weight to the dirt, and he groaned.

"Mister?" Sarah felt strangely shy, and helpless. For a long time she stood staring down at him.

He moaned again. Feeling she had to do something, anything, she rolled him over on his back and looked into his face.

A rough growth of beard was on his jaws, and he looked ill. Sarah felt panic welling up in her, and she realized suddenly that this man had been shot.

"Mister, can you hear me?"

His eyes opened then, lined with pain, bloodshot. "I hear you. . .I'm shot, lady."

"I know—what can I do?" For some unaccountable reason she felt as if she might cry.

"Can you help me inside—got to have water, rest. . ."

Never before had she taken a stranger into her house, but never before had she encountered one who looked so frighteningly close to death.

"Yes, but you'll have to stand. There's no way I can carry you."

He moaned and shut his eyes. "I can stand, if you'll help me."

Trembling with fear and cold, Sarah reached down and grasped his hand. He strained upward, groaning as he sat up, then weakly he struggled to his feet. Growing even paler, he leaned against the saddle for support.

"Can you make it?" Sarah asked, her voice quaking.

"Yeah. . .just help me."

"Lean against my shoulder—careful."

Her fear was forgotten now, covered over by concern for this man's welfare. She put her arm around his waist, supporting him as best she could, leading him toward the steps. With several groans and winces of pain he struggled up onto the porch, then through the door.

"This way, mister. You need to lay down."

He leaned increasingly against her as they moved toward the bed in the corner. She tried to ease him down very gently, but he went suddenly weak and collapsed onto it. She lifted his legs up onto the soft straw tick, then worked at removing his boots.

He breathed a little easier as he relaxed on the tick, but still he looked pale, and he seemed to be fluctuating between consciousness and a sort of swoon. She eyed the bloody shirt. It would have to come off, and the wound would surely need cleaning.

She picked up a pair of scissors and began snipping away at the clotted fabric. The man stirred and came back to consciousness.

"Much obliged, ma'am. Don't think I could have made it."

"What's your name, mister?"

"Murphy. Willy Murphy." His voice had a strained tone.

11

Murphy. A familiar name, but she could attach no particular significance to it. "How did this happen to you?"

He smiled sardonically. "No matter. Let's just say I had a little family disagreement."

She frowned. He was being pretty cagey for a man who might easily be dead if not for her. She realized suddenly that this fellow might be on the wrong side of the law. That realization chilled her. She stopped snipping at the shirt.

"Listen, mister, you better be straight with me. I don't have to keep you here, you know." She was surprised at her own boldness.

He looked at her and sighed with a weak, trembling sound. Then he smiled his strange little smile once more, and nodded.

"I guess you're right. But I have to have your promise that. . .aw, hell, what does it matter. I've had it anyway."

His words confused her, but she sensed that he was about to tell her something she wasn't sure she wanted to hear. But she couldn't afford to be in the dark about this. If someone had done this to him deliberately they might be still on his trail. She could be in danger, just being near this man.

"Lady, I can't expect you to make no promise, but I'd sure be obliged if you didn't go to the law with what I tell you." He paused and looked at her expectantly. She said nothing, and he gave a philosophical grunt. "The law's after me, lady. I was in on a bank robbery in Denver a few weeks back."

Her eyes hardened and her nostrils flared. "Was it a lawman who did this to you?"

He laughed at that. "No way, lady. My brother did it. Can you believe it, my own brother!" He laughed again, as if it was a marvelous joke.

"Why?"

"Because I did something he didn't like. I took the money for myself—never did learn to share when I was a little feller."

"Where is the money?" Sarah felt a sudden embarrassment when he glanced at her with a probing look. "I didn't mean. . .I don't want it for myself. . .oh, blast you, I don't owe you any explanations!"

"No ma'am, I reckon you don't. You might have heard of my brother—he's Noah Murphy."

Her eyes widened and her scalp prickled with fear. My God, she thought, what have I gotten myself into? Noah Murphy is a killer, an outlaw and bank robber! She stared at the man before her, awed and fearful.

"You're one of the Murphy gang—I've heard of you. I didn't recognize your name at first, but now. . .oh, Lord help me!"

"Easy, lady. I ain't gonna hurt you. I don't even have my gun anymore. Besides, I got nothin' against you. I won't even blame you if you go to the law, though I sure hope you don't. It was Noah that shot me. Y'see, I took that cash from the Denver robbery and hid it good, where nobody can find it. Noah didn't like that, and he showed me that with a bullet. I barely got away from him. Thought I would die before I found some place to rest. If it wasn't for you and your place here I might be out there freezin' to death right now."

"Glad I could help." The words sounded very uncertain.

"I ain't gonna stay here long, lady. So don't you worry none. I'll be on my way long before Noah gets on my trail. I just need a little rest, and some food, if you can spare it."

"You need a doctor."

" 'Fraid not, ma'am. Y'see, doctors ask questions,

then they go to lawmen. I can't afford to have nothin' like that—you understand?''

"I understand you'll die if you don't get that slug out of you."

"Better to die than to rot away in some prison. You just leave me to rest, ma'am. I'll be out of your way before sundown tomorrow."

"You need a doctor, mister. Old Doc Hopkins is a good man—you can trust him."

"No." His voice frightened her. Something like anger burned in his eyes, and he spoke the word forcefully.

She drew away. "All right, then. But if you die you can't blame nobody but yourself."

He lay back. "Oh, I don't know—seems to me that ol' Noah had a little somethin' to do with it." Within moments he was asleep.

Sarah cooked up some broth and made hot coffee. When she awoke him about an hour later he was hot as if with fever, and he could only take a small amount of the soup. The coffee he finished, then lay back once more into a fitful slumber.

It was dark outside, and the wind was howling. Sarah kept a fire burning. She couldn't rest—the man was in her bed, and she was too keyed up to relax anyway. She sat at her window and stared out into the darkness.

Fine flakes of snow swirled about, coming to rest on the frozen earth, settling on the woodpile. It might be sooner than she had expected that the first real blizzard came. When that happened travel would be difficult. She might be stranded here in this house, alone with this wounded evil man, waiting for the sound of horses outside that would signal the arrival of Noah Murphy.

The sun had hardly arisen the morning after before she was on the road to Dry Creek. The decision had been made sometime after midnight, as she sat and watched the pale face of Willy Murphy in the darkness,

14

watching his weak breathing and fitful tossing. He was a criminal, a self-confessed bank robber, and she had no obligation to do anything other than provide him shelter until the law could take him to where he belonged. And in Dry Creek the law was Charley Hanna. She would see him, tell him what had happened, and in the company of Doc Hopkins, he could go with her back to the cabin. She would get this outlaw out of her life before anything happened—particularly before Noah Murphy arrived, materializing out of nowhere like a frost-laden death-wind from the mountains.

The cold town of Dry Creek had barely stirred to life when she rode into the street. Smoke rose from every chimney, and she could smell the aroma of sizzling bacon and boiling coffee. Her stomach was empty, but she ignored the rumblings and made her way to the jail-house.

What would Charley Hanna think, seeing her coming in so early? She wondered if he realized how he made her heart race whenever she saw him striding down the street, tall and powerful. She was sure he shared none of the same thoughts about her. Charley seemed to be a man with little time for women, and little interest in them. If he had a woman at all it was Katherine Denning, who cared for Charley's ailing mother. There had been occasions when Sarah had seen Katherine looking at Charley in a way that clearly showed how she admired him. It didn't seem that Charley ever noticed those looks, but one day he surely would, and then he would be gone as far as Sarah was concerned. She hoped that day would never come, for she felt toward him just as she had her husband John in the days they were courting. But it looked as if hers was a love that was to remain hidden and unfulfilled, and she forced herself to accept the fact.

But she couldn't suppress the shiver of anticipation

that went through her as she stepped onto the jailhouse porch and knocked on the door. When she heard the latch opening she smiled to herself.

Her face fell when Bo Myers opened the door. The young deputy grinned at her through a scruffy beard. His teeth were yellow, with prominent gaps between them. When Bo had a rotten tooth, he didn't go to the doc to get it pulled, he just let nature take its course until the tooth was gone. A true man of the earth, this Bo Myers, and he smelled and looked the part. Sarah wondered how Charley could put up with him.

"Hello, Bo. Is Charley in?"

"Yep. Come on in, Miss Reddin'. Charley's over here eatin' breakfast."

Sarah stepped inside and Bo shut out the cold wind. Sarah smiled at Charley, who rose from his chair behind the desk, wiping a trace of gravy from his mustache. She noticed that he looked weary, and his eyes appeared sad.

Chapter 2

Charley looked at Sarah with that same clumsy little-boy expression that marked all of his meetings with women. She smiled at him, also feeling a bit awkward. Bo just kept on grinning his yellow, snaggle-toothed grin.

"Hello, Sarah. Didn't expect to see you so early this mornin.' "

"Hello, Charley. That breakfast smells good."

Charley jumped toward the pot-bellied stove. "Well, here—have some bacon and coffee. Bo, fry up an egg or two for Sarah, here."

"No. . .no, that won't be necessary. I'll eat later. I guess I came to see you on business." She recalled Charley's mother was sick—maybe that was why there was such a sadness deep in his eyes. She asked about her.

"Ma ain't doin' too good, Sarah. Doc Hopkins don't expect her to live too long, though he says he can't tell nothin' for certain. I'm worried about her pretty bad."

"I'm so sorry. Mrs. Hanna has always meant a lot to everybody in Dry Creek. She'll get better—you'll see."

"Thank you, Sarah. I sure hope you're right." Charley smiled, and Sarah felt a warmth steal over her.

"You say you have business. Somethin' wrong out your way?"

Sarah grew serious. Talking to Charley had almost made her forget why she had come. The memory of

17

Willy Murphy came back, and her stomach knotted.

"Yes, I've got trouble, Charley. You're the only one who can help." Charley looked at her blankly, then with increasing concern as she outlined what had occurred. When she mentioned the name of Noah Murphy he exhaled sharply and creased his brow in a frown.

"Good Lord—just what Dry Creek needs. I heard the Murphy brothers had been involved in that Denver bank robbery, but I had no idea they had come up this way. That's the blasted trouble about living up here in the mountains—every outlaw that wants to hide out heads right up here. You say it was Noah who shot Willy?"

"That's what he said."

"How bad hurt is he?"

"It looks pretty bad. That's why I want to get Doc Hopkins to go along with us. The man isn't in any shape to ride. I brought my wagon into town. I figure maybe we can ride him back on that."

"Yeah—good idea. It's a good thing you came, Sarah. Men like Willy Murphy belong in a cell, not the home of a nice, God-fearin' lady like you."

Charley rose from his chair and began strapping on his gunbelt. How tall he was! And handsome! And with his gun strapped to his thigh he appeared deadly and powerful. It was good to know that Dry Creek was under the protection of a man like Charley Hanna. Sarah recalled seeing his father when she was but a girl. Charley was the very image of him, almost like a reincarnation. A strong and able man. As she looked at him her fears of the Murphy brothers diminished, then virtually disappeared. With Charley Hanna along, she would be safe.

"Bo, I'll need you to stay here and look out for things while I'm gone." Charley put on his hat.

"Dang, boss, nothin' will happen around here. It

18

never does. You might need a little help with that Murphy feller. Let me go with you, and—"

"No, Bo, I need you here. There won't be no trouble from nobody as hurt as Willy Murphy. We'll be back here in no time, so you just sit tight."

Charley pulled on a heavy leather coat, lined with fur around the neck, and on his head he sat a battered, weathered old hat that had become so identified with him that most people viewed it simply as an extension of him. He put his hand on Sarah's shoulder and guided her out the door. At his touch she felt the same thrill of warmth as before, and she smiled.

The air was cold and laden with the hint of increasing snow, but Sarah didn't notice. Walking beside Charley toward Doc Hopkins's office made her feel almost giddy like a love-struck young girl. She was not under any illusions—she knew that Charley had no interest in her any more than any other woman in the community—but still she relished this chance to be near him, and she cherished the idea of being able to walk close beside him. She tried to suppress the smile that continually tried to escape from her heart and display itself on her face. After all, this was serious business they were on, and she couldn't afford to let Charley suspect she was thinking of anything other than the matter at hand. For occasionally she did allow herself the privilege of thinking that some day he just might take a second look at her, so she certainly didn't want to scare him away.

They found Doc Hopkins sipping a cup of coffee beside a roaring fire. He welcomed them in cordially, doing his best to silence the coughs that racked his body at intervals.

"Coffee, folks? It's good and hot."

"No thanks, Doc. We've got business with you, pretty serious business," said Charley.

19

"A man's been shot," Sarah explained.

Doc Hopkins's eyes opened a bit wider. "Well, now, that *is* serious. Huntin' accident?"

"No. And it ain't just any man, either. It's Willy Murphy."

Doc looked blankly at Charley. "Who?"

"Willy Murphy, Doc. One of the Murphy brothers—Noah's brother."

Doc nodded sharply then, and his mouth dropped open. "I'll be dagnabbed. Of all things—where is he?"

"That's a story I think I'll let Sarah tell," said Charley. "Go on, Sarah—just like you told me."

Sarah once again ran through her story, and Doc Hopkins was a good listener. He nodded and frowned, grunting with interest at particular details. Hardly had she finished before he was up, gathering items into his medical bag, reaching for his hat and coat on the wall pegs.

"I guess we better get movin'," he said. "I'll patch him up good enough so you can put him behind bars, Charley. That is, if he ain't dead yet."

"That he might be, Doc. I wouldn't be surprised at all."

Charley started to head for the stable to get his horse, then he thought better of it. "I'll just ride along with you, Sarah. Ain't no need for anything other than your wagon, I don't reckon."

Sarah's heart leaped at the prospect of riding all the way back to the cabin sitting right up next to Charley. He crawled up onto the driver's side of the bench and took the reins in his big, rugged hands. Sarah climbed up beside him, and for a moment he looked strangely embarrassed. Sarah knew why—he was aware that he had completely overlooked performing the gentlemanly duty of helping her up into the seat, leaving old Doc Hopkins to perform the task. Not that Sarah cared. She

20

understood that Charley had been given few lessons in the social graces in his life. He meant well, and that was what counted. She took advantage of the fact that Doc Hopkins's wide rump required a lot of room on the seat, and she sat as closely as possible to Charley. He pretended not to notice, but she suspected he did.

The big wagon clattered down the street and out of town. At the other end of the street Kathy Denning stared through a curtained window with cold eyes, watching with scorn as Sarah Redding sat snuggly beside Charley. Her hand released the curtain, and she turned back into the chilly room, her mind racing and her eyes trying to hold back tears.

Charley whistled as he drove the team, but Sarah could tell he was nervous. About a half-mile out of town he began talking about the Murphy boys.

"Those two are a rough pair," he said. "Twin boys, both of 'em mean as snakes since they was little. They took it from their daddy. Pa talked about old Jack Murphy a lot—'Lead Jack,' they called him. Laid claim to a fast gun and an ornery disposition. Pa never met him—said if he had it might have come to a shootout, Pa bein' a lawman and all, and Pa admitted Lead Jack was one gunfighter he wasn't sure he could beat. Me and him talked about Lead Jack and his type a lot, but never around Ma. It seemed to bother her somehow. Lead Jack wound up on the end of a rope. That's exactly where Willy and Noah belong too—Noah worse than Willy, from what I hear. It's a shame there had to be two of them boys—double trouble, y'know."

"Do you think Willy will give us any trouble, Charley?" asked Doc. "I'll do my best to help you if he does, but I'm an old man, and don't even carry a gun."

"No—I think he'll come along quiet. Besides, he's wounded, and Sarah said he didn't have no gun. To be honest, I kinda think we might find him dead."

"Sounds likely to me. A body wound like that can take a man slow and painful. I've seen plenty of 'em in my day." Doc slowly shook his head.

Both Sarah and Charley knew that Doc meant what he said. He had led a rough-and-tumble life amid the wildest mining towns and cattle camps throughout the region, patching up wounds, taking his pay in whiskey and chickens as often as in cash, and moving on from town to town like a drifter. It was only when age started putting rust on his joints that he finally settled down in Dry Creek. He had become a close friend of the Hanna family, as well as everyone else in the town. And no one doubted any time that they could rely on old Doc to come whenever he might be needed. In the years he had resided in Dry Creek he had become something of a community mentor, a respected man just as much as if he had lived there all of his life. He had brought much of the younger Dry Creek population into the world.

The talk continued for the duration of the trip, until at last they reached the bend of the road. Sarah felt her breath quickening, and again she thought of Noah Murphy.

Charley pulled the hay wagon to a stop barely out of sight of the house. Sarah looked at him expectantly.

"I'll go on in from here alone," he said. "If you hear me holler bring the wagon on in." Sarah nodded.

"Charley, I'll go on in with you," Doc said. "If you think there's goin' to be trouble then you might need somebody along."

"No thanks, Doc. There wouldn't be much you could do without a gun. And I would rather have you here with Sarah, anyway."

"Whatever you say, Charley."

"Charley?"

"Yes, Sarah?"

"Please be careful."

"I always am."

He climbed down from the wagon seat and hitched up his trousers before striding firmly toward the bend of the road. Sarah and Doc watched him pause and peep around the trees, then continue. Sarah noted grimly that he loosened the leather thong holding his pistol in the holster.

The house was silent as Charley approached. He didn't know whether to take that as a good sign or an omen of danger. But there was nothing to do but continue.

No smoke came from the chimney. The place looked deserted. Charley felt a keen sense of apprehension nonetheless, and he continued with the utmost caution. His boots made a crackling sound as they trod on the ice coating the ground. Fresh snow was lightly falling, and the wind whistled around the eaves of the cabin.

Charley looked at the windows. No sign of movement inside—no movement of the curtains nor hint of a passing body in the darkness of the cabin interior. Charley still proceeded slowly, his hand inches from the butt of his pistol.

He reached the door. The cabin was as silent as death. Carefully he reached out to the latch, caught it, and lifted it gently.

The door opened onto a dark cabin, the last coals of the fireplace casting a red glow across the floor. Still no sound.

Charley stepped inside, drawing his pistol at the same time. He looked around the interior of the cabin, searching for Willy Murphy.

He was there, still in the bed. Charley frowned. The man was still—too still. Dead?

He moved over to the bed and looked down into the bearded face. There was still a hint of breath about him, and a trace of color in his cheeks. He wasn't dead, but

23

he didn't appear far from it.

Charley returned to the door and stuck his head outside.

"It's all right! C'mon in."

The big wagon clattered around the bend scarcely a second later. Sarah was at the reins. She pulled the wagon into the cabin yard like an expert, then climbed quickly down and darted toward the cabin. Doc Hopkins was a bit slower, having to pause midway down to quell a fit of coughing.

"Charley—is he still alive?" Sarah looked at him with wide eyes, and for a moment he was struck with the realization that this was a very pretty young lady. Funny he had never noticed it before.

"Yeah—but barely, if I read things right. Doc, I think you better take a look at him pretty quick before we lose him. Not that it would be much of a loss, mind you, but I wouldn't mind finding out where he hid that bank money. It'll need to be returned."

"I'll check him out. Sarah, this cabin feels like the inside of a polar bear den. Reckon you could stir up a little fire?"

"Sure thing." Sarah moved quickly inside, followed by Doc. She picked up several small sticks from the pile of wood beside the fireplace and tossed them onto the hot coals. Taking an iron poker in her hand, she began shifting the coals around until the wood caught fire. Quickly she began laying larger pieces of wood atop the smaller ones. Within moments she had burning what promised to be a roaring fire.

Doc Hopkins had moved over to the bedside and was examining the wound in Murphy's side. The man was unconscious, but Charley noted his eyelids flutter as the doctor probed the ugly bullethole. He hoped the outlaw would come around so he could question him.

"That's a bad wound. A .44 shell did it," Doc said.

"I'll need to dig out that bullet."

"Can he take it, Doc? He looks like much pokin' around in that wound might kill kim."

"That it might. But I don't have any choice. If that bullet don't come out he won't live to see sundown. Every time he moves it digs in a little deeper, does more damage. It'll kill him really quick if it stays in. Sarah, boil me up some water, would you? I need to sterilize my instruments."

"Are you going to do it here, Doc? Maybe we could take him back into town."

"No. That would kill him, I'm afraid—well, I'll be! I think he's comin' around a bit!"

Charley moved over to the bedside. Doc was right—Willy Murphy was moving about a little, his mouth opening slightly, his eyelids squeezing shut as if with pain. Then he settled back, moaned, and relaxed a bit. Charley thought he was drifting back deeper into his swoon, but the young outlaw's eyes slowly began to open and stare blankly at the ceiling.

"Hello, boy. I'm a doctor. I'm here to help you."

Murphy's eyes darted quickly to the doctor's face, staring in surprise at the old man. He noticed Charley too, and the lawman watched as the young man's eyes dropped to the badge on his vest. Slowly he began to smile.

"She went and did it anyway," he said. "I ain't surprised."

"It's a good thing, too," Doc Hopkins said. "You're on a straight course to a tombstone unless we do a little diggin' in you."

"Let me talk to him, Doc."

"Make it quick, Charley. There ain't time to waste."

Charley sat down on the bedside and looked sternly at Murphy. He felt vaguely sorry for the young man, but he rarely wasted much sympathy on men known to be

25

thieves and quite possibly murderers.

"I'm Charley Hanna, town marshal for Dry Creek. I know who you are and why you were shot. And I'll tell you straight, boy, it don't look like you have too good a chance to hang around this ol' world much longer. So how about you tell me where you hid that money so I can return it."

Murphy laughed, and it obviously caused him pain. "I'll bet you want to return that money, Mr. Lawman. I'll just bet you do. I never saw a badge-toter yet that wouldn't do his best to cash in on the work of us honest robbers. You can go to hell, mister."

Charley's hand came down in a ringing slap across the young man's jaws. The doctor protested, but Charley silenced him with an uplifted hand.

"Listen, boy, I ain't gonna waste time with you. I oughtta shoot you where you lay just like you was a wounded horse. Lord knows that's what you deserve. You'd best think twice before you sass me, boy. It ain't gonna do you no good. You're half dead already."

"Charley—you keep talkin' like that and you'll be half responsible for his death," Doc cut in. "In a case like this half of the feller's chance depends on whether or not he believes he can make it."

"Frankly, Doc, I don't care if this feller makes it. In fact, the world would do better without him. But I want to get that money back where it belongs."

Murphy's eyes went dull, and his lids closed. Charley cursed softly and frowned. "All right, Doc. Go to work."

Doc Hopkins sterilized his instruments and set immediately to work. Charley moved over to the fireside where Sarah stood, a strange look on her face.

Charley looked at her, then smiled. "I know what you're thinkin'—you're thinkin' I was awful rough on a feller who probably is dyin'. Am I right?"

Sarah smiled almost sadly, and gave a weak nod. It didn't seem right, seeing someone she admired as much as Charley being so rough on a wounded man.

"I'm sorry you had to see that. But y'see, I know the Murphy boys for what they are. They come close to killin' a friend of mine a few years back. He was a farmer on down the valley a ways, and all he was tryin' to do was keep 'em from carryin' off his daughter. She was a pretty lady, and men like that have no scruples about what they do to pretty ladies. They shot him. What they did to the girl I couldn't say to a lady like you. You see why I was so rough on him?"

Sarah made no response, but there was thoughtfulness deep in her eyes. And the hurt and condemnation had faded away from her face.

Charley moved over to the stove. Sarah had built a fire in it, too, and coffee boiled on the top. Charley helped himself to a cup, asking Sarah if she cared for any of the fragrant brew. She shook her head.

Willy Murphy was moaning and crying, and Doc was continuing the operation relentlessly. Years of experience had taught him that such things were best dealt with quickly, for continued and protracted pain was often as deadly as the bullet itself. He was fearful for this young man's life, though. The bullet was lodged deep, and he was certain that vital organs had been damaged. And he couldn't be positive he was making things any better by his own digging.

Sarah wanted desperately to shut out the pain-filled moans of the young man, but there was no way. She moved over to the window and looked outside. The snow was increasing, the flakes larger. The sky was a leaden gray, and the wind had increased, whipping the falling flakes into swirling, intricate patterns before releasing them to blanket the earth. This was not to be a passing storm. Winter had set in completely, sending the snow as its herald.

She stayed by the window even after the operation was over and the moans had ceased. Behind her Doc Hopkins was wiping the blood from his fingers on a scrap of cloth and Charley had moved over to his side.

"Is he goin' to make it, Doc?"

The old man said nothing, but firmly shook his head.

Charley glanced down at the face of Willy Murphy. The color was almost entirely gone now. Even a man with no medical knowledge could feel the death hovering close by, waiting to descend.

"And he never told where the money was."

"Charley?" Sarah's voice had a frightening tone, a tone of warning.

"Yeah?"

"Outside—riders are coming this way."

Charley stepped quickly to the window. Outside the swirling snow was like a white curtain, making vision difficult, masking the road beyond. But through gaps in the storm Charley could make out three horsemen approaching, their shoulders slumped and their hats pulled low against the wind and snow. Charley's knuckles whitened as he clenched his fists, for even through the storm he could recognize the lead rider. He had seen his picture many times, once in a photograph and other occasions on wanted posters.

"Doc, we got trouble. That's Noah Murphy out there."

Sarah went pale and Doc Hopkins muttered something unintelligible.

Chapter 3

The riders stopped within twenty feet of the cabin, Noah Murphy in the middle. Slumped forward with forearm cocked across his saddlehorn he was the image of cocky self-assurance.

"Willy boy! You can come out. We know you're here."

Charley cracked the door and called out through the opening, "Who are you? Ain't no Willy here!"

"Like hell! We know he's in there, and we want him. Ain't none of your affair, buddy. Just send him out and we'll leave you alone."

"There ain't no Willy here, I tell you! Ain't nobody here but me and my brothers. Now, we ain't got no quarrel with you—don't even know who you are, but if you want to miss out on a fight you'd best move on!"

"Buddy, I know there ain't nobody in there but you, a lady, and an old man. We ain't fools—we been watchin' you a good while. We trailed Willy this far—and you'd best send him out."

"Noah Murphy, this is Charley Hanna, marshal of Dry Creek. I've given you a chance to get away without trouble, but you're makin' me lose my patience. Now I've got five deputies in here with me, and we're ready to shoot. You got ten seconds to move your butt or take your weight in lead. I'm countin' now. . .one. . ."

The men looked at each other and smiled, as if

Charley was a child they found very amusing. But the count continued.

"Three. . .four. . ."

Charley was moving his position, heading toward the window. He clasped his pistol and drew it quietly from its holster. Outside the smiles continued, but Charley could note a look of growing nervousness in the riders alongside Murphy.

"Seven. . .eight. . ."

Charley was crouched down low now, his finger on the trigger. His free hand motioned for Sarah and the Doc to hide themselves on the other side of the bed where Willy Murphy lay. They obeyed. Sarah was frightened, yet also intrigued. What was Charley going to do against three armed riders?

Outside the smiles had faded, and hands were creeping toward gun butts.

"Nine. . .*ten!*"

In tandem with the final count Charley's gun whipped forward, smashing the glass out of the window only a fractional second before exploding in a burst of deadly fire. There was a cry outside from one of the riders with Noah Murphy—but not because the shot had struck him. He cried out as he saw his partner pitch backward out of the saddle, his throat bloody and shattered from the .44 shell that had passed through it like an eagle's wing slicing air.

Noah Murphy was aghast. "Well, I'll be. . ." He whipped out a black Colt .44 and sent a shot winging toward the cabin window just as his surviving partner took a shot in the shoulder. The struck man grunted and cursed, letting his pistol fall from a suddenly weakened hand.

"Let's move!" Murphy sounded the cry like a battle call, wheeling his horse around and heading off toward the bend of the road and safety.

The wagon remained where Sarah had left it, and the frightened team hitched to it decided to move at precisely the moment Murphy attempted his escape. The outlaw found his exit suddenly blocked.

A string of vile curses poured from his lips, and expertly he pulled his mount up short. His partner was forced backward suddenly, his horse rearing. With one hand gripping his wounded arm and his horse throwing him suddenly off balance, he crashed from the saddle to the earth. Murphy's horse leaped over the prone man just as one of the Charley Hanna's slugs knocked the outlaw's hat off his head and into the snow-filled wagon. The fallen outlaw was up, racing for his horse, crying out in fear and frustration. The animal darted out of his reach, and the desperate man lunged for the pistol he had dropped when Charley's shot struck him.

Charley waited just long enough for the man to start swinging the pistol around toward the cabin before he put his last bullet into the man's chest. The man jerked once, twice, then stilled suddenly, a crimson stain running out into the snow.

Murphy was gone, but Charley took no chances, emptying out the chamber of his pistol and quickly reloading before standing a wary sentry duty at the window for almost five minutes, becoming at last convinced that the outlaw truly was gone. Only then did he reholster his pistol.

Sarah and Doc Hopkins stood slowly, both shaken, Sarah far worse than the old man. It was the first time she had seen a gun battle; for the doctor it was merely the first time in several years. He had seen plenty of action in his day, and he sent a smile of ungrudging admiration at the marshal.

"Good job, Charley. You just did your Pa right proud."

"Thanks, Doc. You okay, Sarah?"

31

"Y-yes. I think so—yes, I'm all right. My God, are they dead?"

"I reckon so. 'Cept for Murphy. He made it out of here alive."

Doc let Willy Murphy's wrist drop limply from his grasp. "There's one Murphy that didn't. This boy's dead."

Sarah wrapped her arms around herself and walked over to the corner of the cabin, fearing to look either at the dead body of Willy Murphy or the two dead gunmen outside. She was glad she had eaten no breakfast; right now she probably would lose it.

The crowd gathered around the wagon that drove into the snowy streets of Dry Creek. Few words, many gasps and pointing fingers, a crowd of curious and shocked people who stared in silence at the three dead bodies in the back. Charley Hanna drove, and his features were stony. Doc Hopkins was on the other end of the seat, and between them Sarah Redding rode, her shoulders straight and her expression cold; only the faint trembling of her lip and the red rims of her eyes betrayed the tears that were, with effort, held back from release.

By the time the big wagon had reached the marshal's office the crowd was muttering among itself, and mothers were holding trembling hands over the eyes of young children, trying to block out the horrible sight of the stiff, snow-dusted bodies in the back of the wagon.

Fred Colestone was the first to speak to the marshal, now descended from the wagon seat and helping Sarah down after him.

"Who are they, Charley?"

"Don't know who two of 'em are. Skinny one's Willy Murphy. The other two rode with his brother Noah."

"You don't mean to tell me! You done shot it out

with Noah Murphy and his brother? Almighty heaven. . ."

The muttering rose to a faint rumble of amazed voices, and the crowd shifted forward to gaze with a new sense of fascination mixed with repulsion upon the frozen dead forms. Old May Wirt began to sway and lowly sing a hymn, something about crossing the river and what would I find beyond, Oh Lord. No one paid attention to her.

"What happened, Charley?"

"Willy there got shot by his brother, wandered into Sarah's cabin. We went out there to patch him up and bring him in, and he didn't make it. Noah showed up before we could get away. This is the result." He motioned toward the bodies.

"How'd you manage to stand up to three of 'em?"

"I got lucky."

"Why did Noah shoot his own brother?"

Charley didn't answer that one. Instead he moved toward the office door, where Bo was standing open-mouthed, gaping at the dead men. "Bo, I got you a job. Go get Duncan to take care of the buryin'. No need for a funeral that I can see."

"Yessir, Mister Charley." Bo stepped down from the porch and moved toward the office of Duncan, the town undertaker. He paused briefly by the wagon to cast a last look at the dead forms, now turning a rather unattractive blue. Slowly he shook his head and sauntered on down the snowy dirt road.

"C'mon, folks. Ain't no show," Charley said. "Let's move on."

There was no response from the group, who had moved even closer to the wagon. Some were even reaching out to touch the cold bodies, then withdrawing their hands as if from a hot stove.

"Are you all deaf? I said move on!" He got a

response that time, as well as a few stern glances. The residents of Dry Creek were not the sort to like being ordered by anyone, even so respected a man as Charley Hanna. But no one voiced a complaint, for Charley stood too tall, too packed with muscle, for anyone even to consider that. Slowly the crowd dispersed. Charley stood like some angry god on the porch until the last man had gone out of sight, then he turned to enter the jailhouse, where Doc Hopkins and Sarah were waiting. For many minutes the street was empty and silent.

Across the street Bo Myers emerged from the door of the undertaker's establishment and headed back across the street toward the jail. Again he paused at the wagon, stared with fascination at the cold bodies, then stepped up onto the porch and reached out for the door latch.

He stopped when Charley's voice reached him from inside the building.

"No one must know about Noah and that hidden money, you understand? There's folks hereabouts that are greedy enough to turn a little dishonest, maybe go out and do a little prospectin' for that cash. That money belongs in Denver, and if there's any way to get it back there I plan to do it. And Sarah—you'll be needin' to stay here in town instead of back at the farm. Noah probably is sure that all of us know where that cash is hidden, since we spent time with his brother. And he probably doesn't know for sure that Willy's dead. You can bet that those two with him weren't his whole gang. We're in a pretty tight situation, folks."

There was a silence, finally broken by Doc. "You mean you think Noah Murphy might do somethin' against the town?"

"I can't see it any other way, Doc. He wants that money, and here in Dry Creek are the only folks he thinks can lead him to it. He'll be here, soon. I'd be willin' to stake my life on it. In fact, I guess that's just what I'm doin!."

"Charley, that scares me. I don't like to hear you talk like that."

"It scares me too, Sarah. But it's logical. We got real trouble."

"Charley—maybe somebody could get down through the pass and get a little help up this way. We might need it if it comes down to fightin'."

"Doc, you know the pass is snowed under, and with that new snow comin' down there ain't no way anybody could get through. We're stuck up here—alone."

Outside Bo hugged his ear up to the door, straining to hear more.

"Charley, you really think it might come to fighting?"

"Sarah, I'm afraid that's just what will happen."

"Pardon me, Charley—but I think the folks here have a right to know what might happen. It's their necks that are on the line, after all."

"I know, Doc. I'll tell 'em, too. But I want to be the one. It's part of my responsibility, and if there's any hard feelin's about it I want them directed at me, not you two."

"I'll stand beside you, Charley. It won't bother me a bit."

"Nor me."

"I 'preciate it. I really do. But let's do this my way."

"Whatever you say, Charley. I'll go along."

"Thanks a lot, Doc."

"Charley, if I stay in town, where can I live? I don't have any money, so I can't rent a room."

"There's an extra room at my mother's house. You can stay there, free. Kathy will be glad to have the company."

Sarah doubted that very much. But she held her tongue. Charley's words had filled her with fear, and she was even willing to spend time in the very home of her chief rival in order to escape the horror of having to spend lonely days and nights in her own cabin, wondering all the while when Noah Murphy would show up, demanding information she did not have, threatening her with death or maybe even things she would dread far worse than that.

It was that moment that Bo chose to enter, deliberately making as much noise as possible, giving as best he could the impression that only then had he walked across the street and onto the porch. He was greeted by three serious faces and a deadly silence. Muttering to Charley that the undertaker would take care of the dead outlaws momentarily, he retired to his small chamber off the side of the main office, smiling to himself, congratulating himself for what he thought was a very clever piece of detective work, basking in the luxury of secret knowledge.

Doc Hopkins rose. "I'm goin' over to check on your ma. I'll see Sarah over that way, if you got things to do here."

"No—I'll go with you, Doc. I'll need to explain to Kathy about Sarah stayin' with us. Let me get my hat."

The three left, and Bo emerged from his room. He walked to the side window and watched the trio move down the street toward the home of Charley's mother. He had a firm, knowing smile. The snow was falling furiously now, the streets blanketed with at least five inches of the stuff, and there was no sign of a let-up.

Kathy was in the bedroom with Ma Hanna when the three entered. She came to the bedroom door, smiled at Charley and the Doc, and glared with scarcely concealed coldness at Sarah.

"Howdy, Kathy. How's Ma?"

"About the same. You gonna take a look at her, Doc?"

36

"Thought I would. Excuse me." He moved past her to the bedroom door, pulling it shut behind him.

Charley looked very serious, even more than he normally did ever since his mother had taken sick, Kathy noted. And having Sarah alongside him like he did was making her terribly curious. Charley fidgeted, turning his hat in his hands.

"Kathy, there's somethin' I gotta explain about what happened today. There's three bodies down there by the office. And this town may be in for a good bit of trouble. You're the first that's gonna know about it. Sit down, would you? This might take a few minutes to explain."

Kathy obeyed, her heart racing slightly. Something told her she wasn't going to like what Charley had to say.

Martha Hanna's eyes had a dull luster to them, but deep in the orbs Doc could see that rationality still lived in the tired old brain. And he knew that she had finally understood what he had just told her.

"I felt you needed to know. It's been a secret that only we have shared for many years, and frankly I never expected any situation to arise that might make it necessary for Charley to know. But you understand now what might happen if he doesn't learn the truth, don't you?"

Martha Hanna nodded—a barely perceptible movement, but still a nod. Doc noted it, and squeezed her hand.

"Martha, I would be glad to tell him myself, if it would make you feel better. It's going to be hard for you to communicate with him now. You just give me the word and I'll tell him."

The old lady turned her eyes to the old doctor, and he smiled at her with a natural tenderness made all the

37

more mellow by his age. Martha's distorted mouth twisted slightly, and the doctor knew that she, too, had smiled.

"Not. . .yet," she said, the words scarcely understandable, yet clearly comprehended by Doc.

Once more he squeezed her hand. "All right, Martha. You give it some thought. I'll be by to check on you again real soon. You rest now. Goodbye, Martha."

Then he left her alone. She stared up at the ceiling for a long time, her dull eyes thoughtful, misted with a hint of tears. Then her right arm lifted and reached across her chest, stretching toward the beside table and the pad and pen that sat atop it. Only after great and extended effort did she reach it.

Every muscle aching, every nerve at the bursting point, she began to write in a scrawling, almost illegible hand. And as she wrote she began to weep.

Kathy felt only a numbness when she discovered the still, dead body of Martha Hanna laying cold in the bed, the pen still gripped in her hand and the papers scattered before her. Kathy had dreaded this moment, knowing that at almost any time it could come, but now that it had she could feel no sorrow, no pain, nothing.

But her heart had been filled already with intense pain before she entered the room, and almost a hatred for Charley Hanna. For she had seen, through the window of the front room, how Charley had held the pale and shaken Sarah Redding in his arms in the falling snow, and how he had drawn her close to him when she began to cry. Kathy had felt something like a dying in her soul when she saw that, and then the numbness had begun, covering over the pain with a soothing balm of hatred for both Charley Hanna and the blonde Sarah with whom, it seemed, she was going to have to share her very home.

Kathy stood and looked at Martha Hanna's still face for a full minute before she closed the blankly staring eyes and lifted the sheet gently over her face. Then she picked up the papers one by one, arranging them in order, frowning at the rough script. Then she began to read.

Her eyes burned with a new light when at last she finished reading the pages, and slowly a smile stole onto her face. She looked again at the still form on the bed, and this time there was an expression of something like gratitude on her face. The smile beamed down on Martha Hanna's dead body for only a moment, then Kathy turned and entered the empty main room of the house.

With an iron poker she stirred the fire into full blaze, then with a kind of laugh tossed the pages into the flames.

Chapter 4

Bo Myers stood alone on the boardwalk, watching the beckoning glow from the Lodgepole Saloon, listening to the faint tinkling of piano music from the interior of the log building. The street was empty, and white with snow, and it seemed there was nothing for him to do. Charley had told him to go out on patrol, but he circled the entire town three times without finding a thing out of order, and he had no inclination to circle it again.

And anyway, Freddy and Joe Marcus had entered the saloon, and he was dying to join them. They had raised many a ruckus in Dry Creek, those two, and back before he had been deputized Bo had often been right in the midst of it all with them. Now he was supposed to be respectable, the kind of young man folks could look up to and count on, but there were times when the old days called out to him, and the desire for carousing became overwhelming. It was a cold night, and windy, and nothing seemed more inviting than the idea of sipping a good glass of redeye whiskey in the warmth of that saloon, with old friends beside him. He looked across the street at the log building, sadness in his eyes, indecision plaguing him.

Snorting low under his breath, he stepped from the boardwalk to the snowy street and began to stride across toward the welcoming glow. But halfway there he stopped, then sighed with a tone of despair of the sort that can only be mustered by those who are about to forgo the pleasures of vice for the duties of responsibility.

"Bo, you can't go in there," he muttered aloud. "Charley is countin' on you to stay out here on patrol. You know what'll happen if'n you set foot in the Lodgepole."

And that he did. He would sip first one drink, then another, then at last he would be roaring drunk, useless as a lawman. He would let Charley down, and that was one thing he didn't want to do. Charley had taken plenty of kidding for hiring Bo as a deputy in the first place; most folks thought he was a no-account young devil who had not one decent bone in him. But Charley had believed in Bo, and that had meant a lot to the young man. Only a time or two since he was deputized had he yielded to temptation and gotten good and tight.

"No sir," he said once more. "Can't go in there. No sir."

He turned his back on the building, and began walking down the middle of the street, whistling, trying to convince himself that he didn't really want a drink anyway. He made it almost a hundred feet before he stopped, twisted his lips, and shook his head.

"Aw, heck!" And with that he turned and walked straight toward the Lodgepole, his anger at his own weakness increasing with every step, then suddenly dissappearing as soon as he pushed open the door and stepped into the warmth of the saloon.

The place provided a welcome contrast to the cold and snow outside. There were lamps everywhere, so many that the interior was lit almost like main street at noonday. The music was loud, drowning out all thoughts of self-condemnation, and all about was merriment. Bo grinned and tipped back his slouch hat. He would have one drink—one little drink—and then he

41

would return to his duty. After all, every working man needed a break, and who knows—maybe something would happen in the saloon that needed the attention of a lawman.

"Bo! Ol' Bo Myers! Come over here and have a drink! Or do you lawmen not drink booze?"

Bo grinned, then let the grin fade, for he recognized in Joe Marcus's voice that tone he always used when he made fun of Bo's position as deputy. Apparently Joe found it remarkably funny that his old drinking and fighting partner was now a lawman, and there were times when he took advantage of every opportunity to make biting comments on the subject. It irritated Bo to no end, but tonight he would put up with it. He was wanting that drink too bad to turn away now.

"I reckon I'll have a drink if'n I want one," he retorted, imagining his defiant tone to be cutting to Joe. But the young roughneck just grinned all the harder and glanced at his brother. Bo was in true form tonight, and that would provide a good deal of entertainment, Joe was sure.

Bo walked over and sat down beside Joe, snapping his fingers at the bartender. He was determined to act cool and unruffled no matter what kind of ridicule Joe and his brother threw at him. And as Joe looked at the young lawman, he could read that intention as clearly as if Bo had written it across his face.

"What'ya want, Bo?" The bartender had no intention of waiting on tables, no matter how many times Bo snapped his fingers.

"Redeye. A good shot of it, too."

Freddy Marcus chimed in. "Now, Bo, you think you ought to be drinkin' while your on duty? Ol' Charley might not think too highly of that."

"What do I care what Charley thinks? He don't own me, does he?" Bo stood and swaggered over to the bar to take his drink. Pausing uncertainly, he took the bottle, too, knowing full well he was in for trouble. But with Joe and Freddy looking on, he was determined to put on as cocky and self-certain a show as he could.

He plopped back down in his chair and took a sip of the strong liquor. He almost choked on the fiery drink, but he managed to squelch his cough.

"Yessir," he said. "I don't worry none about what ol' Charley thinks. Ain't nobody got a hold on Bo Myers. Nobody at all."

"That ain't what I hear, Bo. I hear you jump when Charley whistles. Hear he's got a ring through your nose right good."

Bo looked up sharply at Joe. His was a weak intellect, and with no physical beauty to speak of, the only thing he had left was pride. And any man that ridiculed him was touching him at his weakest area.

"Joe—if I ever hear any talk like that again I'll bust a few heads!" Bo said. "I don't owe Charley Hanna a thing!"

Rand Cantrell turned around from the bar, a faint smile on his handsome face. He was a tall, lean man, dressed in a sharp suit and cocky hat, and it was the name of Charley Hanna that had drawn his attention. Anything to do with Charley Hanna could get his attention almost anytime.

"Bo, you been involved in some of that lawman work lately? Was it you that got Willy Murphy? I hear ol' Charley managed to do that without any help from you at all!"

"Well, what of it? If'n I had been there there'd be Noah dead beside him. Both you boys know I ain't no slouch with a gun."

Bo refilled his glass and drained the whiskey in one swallow. It was starting to feel good in his gut, and the old craving was growing with every second. He had never been one to stop with one drink—or even three or four.

"That may be so, Bo, but I notice when there's any lawin' to be done Charley leaves you sittin' here in Dry Creek while he goes out and does it hisself. How do you account for that, Bo?"

Bo was starting to get mad now. He tossed down another drink. His throat and chest were feeling warm now, and his brain was quickly being dulled by the powerful liquor. Rand Cantrell looked on, sipping his drink casually. The loud young deputy was amusing to him, but the topic of conversation was not. Rand Cantrell didn't even like to think about Charley Hanna, much less hear talk about him. But it made him feel good to see Hanna's only deputy getting drunk on duty. It made him feel good because he knew that it would make Charley Hanna mad. Charley Hanna was a sore point in the life of Rand Cantrell—a very sore point.

"Listen here, Joe, I'm every bit as good a lawman as Charley Hanna—every bit as good. Charley might think he's better, but ol' Bo knows a lot more than he thinks. Yessir, I know a lot he don't have no idea I do."

Bo threw down another drink, not noticing the new, intensified light of interest that burned in Rand Cantrell's eyes. Indeed, he had not noticed the man at all, leaning up against the bar behind him. Nor had he any idea that his words were increasingly hostile toward Charley Hanna. He was talking under the influence of the whiskey now, concerned with nothing but saving face before the mischievously grinning brothers across the table from him. Neither of them really cared what Bo thought of Charley, or vice versa; their only interest was in goading Bo further into rage simply for the sake of watching him stew. But not so Rand Cantrell. Bo's words had made him realize that the young deputy just might really hold some sort of information that would

44

put Charley Hanna in a bad light. And if so Rand Cantrell wanted to know about it.

Rand Cantrell had not always hated Charley Hanna. There had been a time when he might even have said he liked the man. But that was before the marshal had humiliated him, degraded him before a crowd.

Rand was a gambler, and a good one. But the same deceptive smoothness which made him a winner at the gambling table also had a way of making him enemies. It had only been a few months before that a young drifter had felt the sting of Rand's gambling skill, and like many other hotheads had done in the past, he had sought to even the score with a gun. It had been Charley Hanna that intervened to keep Rand from literally beating the young drifter to death after the gambler kicked a pistol from the young man's hand and torn into him with his fists. Hanna entered the fight, striking Rand right before the assembled, hooting crowd of Dry Creek's saloon patrons, humiliating him. Rand tried to restore his dethroned pride by ripping into Charley like a wildcat, but the marshal beat him off with ease, even smiling while he did it, as if Rand were something funny, something worthy of contempt. That had been more than the arrogant gambler could stand, and he had tucked the injury away in his mind, letting it grow and torment him, making him long for revenge against Charley Hanna.

He poured himself another drink and watched the two Marcus brothers continue their sport with the increasingly drunken deputy. For a full hour they continued, pumping Bo full of liquor, and baiting him with talk of how Charley Hanna was so superior to him, how he danced like a puppet when the marshal gave the slightest tug at the string, how everyone in town laughed about him behind his back and marveled that he would let himself be so continually belittled by Charley Hanna.

Bo at first protested, trying to defend himself, and when the thought struck him, trying to defend Charley also—but at last he stopped talking and started listening. He was drunk now, full drunk, and had been for some time, for he had always been one to feel the effects of liquor almost as soon as it was in his stomach. All thoughts of his planned return to duty were gone; his soul was raging hot and angry within him—angry against the marshal who, according to the Marcus boys, had been ridiculing him behind his back for months. It never crossed his mind that the Marcus boys might be lying to him just to goad him on; he was too drunk and too much a victim of mental sluggishness to realize anything of the sort. The more they drilled their propaganda into his mind, the more convinced he was of its truth. He sat glowering into the corner, sipping his drink slowly now, wondering how he could have been such a fool as to trust Charley Hanna.

The Marcus brothers soon grew tired of their game, for clearly Bo was no longer going to respond. Bidding him goodbye, they donned their ragged hats and dirty coats and stepped out into the night. Rand Cantrell stood in silence at the bar, studying Bo, who was seated now with his head cast down and his eyes burning with deep and solemn thought. Smiling to himself, Cantrell stepped over to the table, a fresh bottle of whiskey in his hand.

"Mind if I sit down, Bo?"

Bo didn't look up, but gestured toward an empty seat. Rand Cantrell sat down, deliberately scooting the bottle in front of Bo's nose.

"Drink?"

Bo looked up then, and smiled. "Thanks. I believe I will."

Rand sipped his whiskey, studying Bo over the rim of his shot glass, his mind whirling. Something in his instincts told him that this young man could provide a key to revenge on Charley Hanna. Rand made his living trusting his instincts, and rarely did they fail him.

"Bo, I heard the Marcus brothers giving you a hard time just now. Didn't seem quite right to me. I bet you know a good deal more about this town and Charley Hanna than you let on. I've always thought that."

Bo looked at the gambler, smiling. After the bruising his ego had taken, he was ready to hear anything that sounded even remotely like praise. And Rand Cantrell was ready to dish it out.

"You got it right. Charley Hanna would be surprised to find out what I know about him. Plenty surprised."

"I'd say he would, Bo. I'd say he would. Here—more whiskey. It's a cold night. You'll need it."

"Thanks a lot, Mr. Cantrell. It is a mite cold."

Cantrell leaned back and watched Bo drain the drink. Things were playing right into his hand—and if he played that hand right, it would be Charley Hanna that would wind up on the worst end of the deal.

"Yessir, Bo, I wouldn't be surprised if you knew a lot of secrets about old Charley—things he might not want spread around. Living with him right there in that office like you do, why, I bet you find out a lot of things."

Bo grinned, his bloodshot eyes shining. "You got it, Mr. Cantrell. Ol' Charley's secrets ain't as secret as he thinks they are. Not a bit."

Rand smiled, deliberately letting his face show intense interest in Bo's words. But the expression faded into a sort of skeptical look, one that did not go unnoticed by Bo.

"Sure, you know things, Bo, but do you know important things? I mean really important things. . .things he keeps secret."

Bo looked disturbed. He had taken enough ridicule tonight, and his liquor-dulled brain sensed that Rand,

47

who he had thought was going to speak words to lift his depressed spirit, was in fact about to turn against him. And at this moment, he wasn't sure he could stand that. He gazed in despair at the growing look of doubt in Rand's eyes, and realized that if he was to save his self respect he would have to do more than claim he was in on the intricate workings and dark secrets of the office of the Dry Creek marshal—he would have to prove it.

"Yeah, I know important things—real important things."

Cantrell leaned forward, his face smirking but a strange eagerness burning almost imperceptibly in his dark eyes.

"Like what?"

Bo licked his lips and looked around him. He leaned forward and spoke in a low, subdued voice.

"Like how Charley was talkin' to Sarah Redding and Doc Hopkins about money hid out in the woods somewhere—and about how Noah Murphy would be ridin' in to find out where it was. I heard 'em talkin' earlier today, just a little after they come in with Willy Murphy and those other fellers. Yessir, I heard it all myself."

Rand Cantrell leaned back, a triumphant smile on his face.

"You don't say. I guess you do know something pretty important, Bo. A lot more important than you might realize. Here—take the bottle, it's yours. You and I need to have us a good talk, Bo—a good long talk."

Bo Myers grinned at his companion, and sensed that he had won. He liked it when people paid attention to him, and talked as if he was important. He liked it a lot, and right now would say almost anything to keep that attention focused on him. His hand tipped the bottle and strong whiskey flowed into his glass. If Rand Cantrell wanted talk, he would get it, plenty of it. Bo drained his glass.

Chapter 5

The skies cleared a little the following day, and for that Charley was glad. It was hard enough to carry his mother to her burial place anyway, and cloudy skies would only have made it worse. The wind was icy cold, though, and the crowd of mourners huddled closely together as they trudged up the small hillside which was marked with rude wooden crosses, hand-engraved tombstones, and an occasional store-bought monument that had been lugged by supply wagon all the way up from Denver. It was a quiet place, a somber place, and with the white blanket of snow over all, the dark and empty grave dug for Martha Hanna gaped like some sort of devouring mouth, a fearful thing. Charley tried to avoid looking at it, but found himself drawn to it nonetheless. He felt he should be crying, but instead he simply felt a coldness inside himself, worse than the physical cold of the biting wind from the mountains.

Virtually the whole town was there, those who had been friends of the Hanna family and those who had cause to hate them. Weddings and funerals always drew a crowd in Dry Creek, for there were few sources of diversion for the townsfolk. But Martha Hanna would have had no lack of mourners anyway; she had been a woman well loved by virtually everyone, even those who hated Charley and his father. Even Rand Cantrell, who lingered toward the rear of the crowd, recognized that

49

she had been a good woman.

Charley had noticed Rand in the crowd of mourners, and was rather surprised that the man had shown up for the funeral. He knew Rand had no love for him—though he was in no way suspicious that the man loathed him as much as he truly did—and he couldn't see why the gambler would suffer the cold wind to see the mother of a man he disliked laid to rest. But Charley did not more than casually ponder the mystery; he was filled with grief, a cold, numb grief, and it shoved all other considerations out of his mind.

Though not entirely. He thought constantly of Noah Murphy, and felt the dread of his possible coming hanging like a suspended blade over his head. He had realized from the moment the burial service was called that this would be the perfect opportunity to tell the people of Dry Creek about the danger they were in, and he fully intended to do so as soon as his mother was properly laid beneath the frozen earth. He didn't look forward to the task, but neither did he dread it, for the death of the woman who had nurtured him from his birth overshadowed all of his feelings, and with her so freshly taken from him he really didn't care what anyone else thought of him. He would tell the people, right here beside the grave, and then preparations could be made for defense against a possible attack.

Preacher Bartlett looked appropriately serious as he waited for the mourners to quit stirring about before he began his eulogy. The coffin, a rude pine box, had been placed beside the open grave, ropes beneath it to make lowering it into the grave a bit easier. The pallbearers were ruddy faced in the cold, and puffed a bit from the exertion of carrying the coffin up the steep, rough slope to the graveyard.

Charley stood beside Kathy, whose eyes were red and stained with tears. She had a disturbed look on her face, but no one thought it unusual. After all, she had nursed Martha Hanna for years now, and it was to be expected that the woman's death would bother her very much. Sarah Redding noticed that she repeatedly cast strange glances toward the big lawman standing beside her, who himself took no notice of the fleeting looks. Charley's face looked weary and almost old in the feeble sunlight, and many in the crowd noticed again the remarkable resemblance the young man bore to his late father, who lay beneath the snow beside the fresh grave which would in minutes receive the body of Martha Hanna.

"Friends and neighbors, we are here gathered to perform the sad duty of returning the body of Martha Hanna to the soil from which she came," began the preacher. "Truly it is a sad duty on this earthly side, for we have all known and loved Martha throughout the years, but let it give us peace to know that even now the angels are rejoicing on that distant shore to welcome the one who has come into their midst. While we moan and cry over our loss, truly the Kingdom of God sings in joy at its gain, and while we stand and shiver in the cold wind of these Colorado hills, surely our friend Martha does stand and enjoy the warmth of the sweet wind that blows across Jordan from the everlasting hills of that blessed land which we all seek. . . ."

Already Charley had let his attention drop away from what the preacher was saying, for he had heard it all before, at other funerals. Through his mind was running a cycle of images, vivid pictures of times past, times when he was young and his mother and father were with him. He saw their faces clearly, unlined with the wrinkles of age, free of the weariness of being old, and the sight touched him. For a moment he was carried back to those days, and it made him happy and sad at the same time. He lifted up his eyes and studied the clouds that floated on the horizon, far above the sharp,

51

snowy peaks of the mountains that loomed majestically around the tiny burial place and the crowd of people. He found himself wishing, as he had many times in youth, that he could soar as the eagle soared above those peaks, to escape for at least a time from the drab, mundane life of this small town, a town which now seemed to him to be a living monument to the one he had lost. The preacher's voice droned on, the words not even registering in Charley's mind.

Doc Hopkins was staring not at the mountains but at the coffin, and his eyes were moist. He had a blank look on his face, and his eyes were dull, as if they were veiled to hide thoughts too deep, too personal, to expose to the world. Occasionally he would cough, and for a moment his old frame would be jolted, his mind flashing back to the reality of the moment, but then the same dull luster would cloud his eye, and again he would be immersed in deep, private thoughts.

It hurt Charley when the last prayer was said and the pallbearers moved to the sides of the coffin. Slowly the coffin was lowered into the hole, creaking and snapping while the men holding the ropes puffed and grunted with their burden. A few ladies of the group struck up a feeble hymn, the music whipping away in the wind as they sang. Charley watched the box lower, and his heart felt like lead.

The sound of sniffling and faint weeping could be heard throughout the crowd. Martha Hanna had been a lady with many friends. Charley had many friends too, yet his hardnosed approach to keeping the peace and the laws in Dry Creek had made him many enemies, too. Some had come out to the funeral along with the friends, standing intermingled among them, faces somber. In all his life Charley had never met anyone who knew Martha and didn't love her.

When the box was lowered Charley did what was

expected of him—he took a shovel, scooped up a bit of dirt, and dropped it onto the coffin. It made a hollow, dull sound, like a final heartbeat punctuating the end of a life.

Then it was over. Martha Hanna's funeral was finished, and she was left to lay silently beside her husband.

But it wasn't over for Charley. The thing he had to tell the crowd came rushing into his mind, and suddenly he was struck with fear. How would the people react? How could he desecrate his mother's burial with such a dread pronouncement, one that could be a sentence of death to an innocent town?

He started to speak, but the words choked in his throat. And before he could force them out, he noticed that all eyes had turned to Rand Cantrell, who had climbed up onto a stump, his hands raised to draw the attention of the crowd.

"What in the devil is he. . ."

Bo Myer's voice came to him from behind, a cracked, hoarse whisper. "Oh, Lord—oh no." Charley turned to the young deputy, frowning, confused. Bo's face was twisted in an expression of guilt and dread, and he was staring at Rand Cantrell.

"Bo, what is this?" Charley asked.

There was no time for an answer, for Cantrell began to speak. His voice was clear and steady, and his expression was serious.

"Friends. . .friends, stop for a moment. I have something to say that all of you should hear. It isn't good, and I know that perhaps so sacred a time as a funeral is not the best time to bring bad news, but I feel I have no choice. Please, don't leave. . .listen. You all need the information I have. It has to do with our own marshal Charley Hanna, money hidden by the Murphy gang, and possible danger to our town."

53

Many faces had expressed irritation at seeing Dry Creek's only professional gambler putting on such an exhibition at the funeral of so respected a lady as Martha Hanna. But when he mentioned the words "money" and "danger," irritation changed to interest, and the restless movement of the crowd ceased.

"What are you talkin' about, Rand?" someone asked.

"I'm talking about a violation of trust, a marshal who deliberately withheld important information from all of us in order to better his own position although it endangered Dry Creek."

"I talked last night to Deputy Bo Myers, and what he had to say bothered me. Deputy Myers overheard Charley, Sarah Redding, and Doctor Hopkins talking in the marshal's office immediately after the bodies of Willy Murphy and his two companions were brought in. He heard Charley talking about money hidden by Willy Murphy, money that his brother Noah wants. He heard Charley tell the others to say nothing about the money to any of us, even though the marshal suspected at the time that Noah Murphy would make some sort of attack upon Dry Creek in order to find out where the money was.

"You see, apparently Noah Murphy is convinced that our marshal and his friends know where that money is hidden. He believes that Willy Murphy revealed that information before he died. And from the secretive way in which the marshal was acting, I suspect that Noah Murphy is right.

"So it looks like Charley Hanna has some explaining to do. Do you deny what I've said, Marshal?"

Bo cut in before Charley could shake himself out of his daze enough to answer. "He's twistin' what I said, Charley. I never meant to. . ."

"Let the marshal answer," Rand interrupted.

Charley felt rage stirring through him, for he realized that Rand Cantrell had placed him in a position from which there was no possible escape. If he said that the gambler was correct about the hidden money, then he would look as if he truly had intended on keeping the affair a secret. To say he was just getting ready to speak when Rand cut in would not sound convincing, in spite of the fact that it was true. And to deny what he said would be equivalent to leaving the town open to attack from the Murphy gang, should such a thing actually occur. And so for a moment he stammered, turning red, and that in itself only lent credibility to Rand Cantrell's statement.

"We're waiting, Marshal."

"You've got yourself a pack of half-truths, Rand. It is true that Willy Murphy talked about hidden money, but he never said where it was. And I had no plans to keep the thing a secret. I would have spoken up just a moment ago if you hadn't jumped up on that stump like a revival preacher. And whether or not Noah Murphy will attack Dry Creek I can't say—that's just speculation. But I did not intend to leave the town in the dark on this, and I sure had no plans for tryin' to find that money myself, if that's what you mean. And if I did find it I would just take it back to Denver where it belongs."

"Is that right, Marshal? If you were going to tell the town about it why didn't you do so when you brought the bodies in? You had a good chance, since half the population was standing around looking at the bodies in the wagon."

Charley could not respond, because he had no clear answer. He had hardly had a chance to think the situation through yesterday when he brought in the bodies, and the idea of informing the town then simply had not crossed his mind. But now that oversight was making him look bad—darned bad.

"Do you really think the Murphy boys will attack the town?" someone asked.

"I hope not," Charley responded. "But Noah Murphy ain't the kind to give in easy when somethin' is taken from him. He just might attack us."

The marshal looked around him at the encircling faces. On them he saw expressions of suspicion, doubt, even sadness in a few cases. In spite of his history of honesty and his fair dealings with all of the townfolk, it was clear that Rand's venom had taken its effect on the people. The seed of doubt had been sown, and there was nothing Charley could do to stop it from growing into full-fledged suspicion.

The crowd began to disperse, moving on down the hillside. Charley watched them leave, his countenance downcast. When he looked at Rand Cantrell he felt a strong surge of bitterness. The gambler had twisted the truth just enough to put Charley into a pinch from which he could not wriggle free.

Sarah moved up beside him. "Some of them may doubt you, Charley, but most of them will stick with you. You'll see."

"I just hope that the town has enough sense to prepare for that possible attack. What I'm afraid of is that they'll get it into their heads to look for that money. And with Noah Murphy around these parts, that could be a deadly mistake. I reckon that's part of the reason that I held off in tellin' 'em about it all—I figured they might get a little greedy. But somehow even that wouldn't have sounded good if I tried to say it. It would only look like I'd got greedy myself and didn't want anybody else to know about that cash."

Bo Myers stood off from Charley, shaken and ashamed, only then realizing what his indiscretion of the night before had done. He had sat and told everything he knew to Rand Cantrell, filling in the gaps he didn't understand with bits and pieces from his own imagination. And Cantrell had taken that already distorted picture of the facts, twisted it diabolically, and used it to good effect against Charley. Bo felt that at that moment he wouldn't be worth the bullet it would take to shoot himself.

The deputy glanced over to where Kathy Denning stood on the edge of the dispersing crowd. She was watching Charley slip his arm around the waste of Sarah Redding, and even in his distraught state Bo noticed the fiery anger that snapped in her eyes. She turned on her heel and walked briskly down the hill.

Billy Tork, who kept the grounds at the church and looked after the cemetery, picked up his shovel and began throwing heaps of dirt mixed with crystaline jewels of ice into the grave while the wind whistled through the over-arching mountains, making a strange, mournful sound.

Chapter 6

Charley knew he had cause to be angry with Bo, but the deputy apologized with such tearful sincerity that the marshal just had to forgive him.

"I'm sorry I ever talked to Cantrell about what I heard, Charley," he said. "But Cantrell didn't tell everything I told him. I told him you were gonna tell the town about it all at the funeral, but he left that out. If you want I'll tell the whole dang town about it."

"Thanks, Bo. But it's too late now. Folks would think I just told you to say it."

Bo retired to his room, and Charley sat brooding. It was dark night outside, and the snow was falling thick and fast. By now there was probably several feet of it blocking the pass through the mountains. Travel was cut off; the town was stranded.

Doc Hopkins had come in earlier with further depressing news, telling how many of the men of the town were preparing to venture out into the mountains in a desperate, greed-inspired search for the money. It was a foolhardy plan, one only money-hungry men could conceive. The odds of finding the money were almost nil, but the lust for easy wealth was overriding all rational considerations.

The worst part of it was that right now the town needed all of its men, for if an attack came, as Charley feared, every man, woman and child in the community would need to take some role in the defense. The exact size of the Murphy gang no one knew, but rumor had it that Noah Murphy at times led almost thirty men, though with Willy and the other two dead, the number was reduced somewhat. But those that remained were trained gunman, ruthless killers, and they would pack as much wallop as a band twice their size. Dry Creek might soon face a seige, and several of its most hardy men were about to take off on a fool's mission for money that wasn't theirs. Charley knew it would do no good to try to convince them to stay behind, so he had no plans to try. Let them go, and those that were left would make their defense as best they could.

Doc had told Charley that many of the townspeople apparently didn't believe Rand's claim that Charley knew where the money was. But they were not convinced that Charley had been preparing to tell them about the threat of the Murphy boys, and many harsh words were being spoken against the marshal because of that. Rand Cantrell's seeds of dissent were springing into bitter blossoms of anger, and later, Charley was sure, the result would be hatred and fear. It was amazing to him that in such a short time a messed-up, ridiculous situation like this could come into being.

Charley realized that Cantrell's words had not been for the sake of the community. Cantrell cared only for himself—Charley had sense enough to know that—and apparently the gambler's dislike for Charley went beyond anything the marshal had guessed. It mystified him somewhat, for he was not himself a vengeful person, and could not really understand those who were. Whatever his motivation, Cantrell had surely managed to get him into a fine mess.

The door opened and Sarah rushed in. Charley could tell immediately that she had been crying.

"Charley, I can't stand it, not for another moment!

I've tried to get along with her, but she won't let me—please, Charley, you've got to get me away from her."

"Sarah, hold on. What are you talkin' about?"

"I'm talking about Kathy, Charley. The things she has been saying about you—I just can't stand it!"

Charley frowned. Kathy? Talking against him? That didn't sound right. Kathy had always been a friend.

"Sit down, Sarah. . .here, sit here. Now just settle down and tell me what the problem is."

Sarah looked at Charley through bleary, tear-filled eyes. She could see the hurt in him, and knew that the strain of facing such a crisis directly after the death of his mother was taking a hard toll on him. Suddenly she felt ashamed that she had come with news that would only make things harder for him. But the way Kathy had been talking, running him down—it was too much to take.

"Charley, Kathy has been awful cold toward me. I didn't expect anything otherwise—we've never been friends, and I know she didn't like the idea of me living with her. And I could stand her unfriendliness, but I can't stand it when she talks against you. She says that Cantrell was probably right about you and that money. She said that you probably killed Willy Murphy yourself after he told you where it was."

Charley was aghast. He couldn't believe that the lady who had taken such good care of his mother for so many years would say such things about him. Not Kathy!

"Sarah—why would she say that? Kathy knows I would never. . ."

"I don't know what she knows, Charley—just what she said. And I can't take it anymore. I'll sleep in the street before I'll stay in the same house with her for another second. I'm sorry. Don't think me ungrateful for your letting me stay there, but it's just getting to be too much."

"I understand, Sarah. But where can you stay if you don't stay there?"

"I'll stay with the Widow Thompkins. We're friends, and she won't care. I think she would like to have the company." Sarah paused, and looked with intense sadness at Charley. "Charley, why are people saying such things? How can they turn against you so?"

"I don't know, Sarah. I figure Rand is mad because I licked him a while back. The other folks, well, they're just ready to talk, to do anything to give a little excitement to their lives, I reckon. Doc says many of 'em don't really believe any of Rand's tales, though I admit it didn't look good for us to have to admit that at least a little of what he said was true. What scares me is that folks seem more interested in tryin' to find that money than preparin' for the fight that's comin'."

"Do you really think that the Murphy gang will come here?" Sarah asked.

"As long as they think there's somebody in this town that can lead them to that money they will. And they won't care how many innocent folks get killed, neither. With the pass blocked we're stuck up here to defend ourselves the best we can. It's gonna to be one devil of a fight, Sarah. I'm sorry I can't get you outta here. I know what the Murphys can do, and I'm dreading it awful bad. They're killers of the worst sort, Sarah. I've never heard of any other gang the size of them, and none are more cruel. I hate for you to have to see what will happen here."

"Charley, is it really as bad as you're making it out? You're scaring me."

"I wish I could say it wasn't, Sarah, but I can't. There was another town they burned a couple of years ago—I was through there about a month after it happened, and folks were still dazed from it all. Almost half of the population was killed, and a lot of property destroyed.

"You see, Murphy's men are almost like a little army, all of 'em vicious. They enjoy seeing people suffering, they enjoy killin' and burnin'. Of all the outlaw gangs that have roamed these mountains, they're about the worst, in my book. Other killers usually have a reason for what they do, but the Murphys look on it as a sport. The slightest provocation can bring them down hard on anybody who gets in their way. And right now it's us—the people of Dry Creek—that they want. I just wish ol' Willy Murphy had died before he ever got to your place. If he had then we wouldn't have to worry about what might happen, I don't believe. I think they would leave the town alone. I hope that they do now."

Outside the office there was the sudden noise of a horseman on the street, riding up fast and hard. Charley tensed. The rider had stopped just outside the office. For a moment there was silence. Sarah looked up into Charley's suddenly intense face, confused.

"Listen to me, Dry Creek!" The shout came from the horseman. Charley moved to the window. The man was sitting astride a big stallion right in the midst of the street, shouting loudly, his message clearly intended for the whole town.

"Listen to me! You have three people in this town who know where the money is that belongs to us! You got two days to turn any one of 'em over to us or you'll all feel what's it's like when Noah Murphy and his boys burn a town! You got that? You turn over Charley Hanna, the old man, or the lady, and we'll let you go. You got two days! And that starts tonight. If we don't have at least one of them three within forty-eight hours you can count on a little visit from the Murphy gang that evenin'. That's the word from Noah Murphy!"

Bo had emerged from the back room, strapping his gunbelt around his waist. Charley directed Sarah to the side of the room, where she crouched behind the desk, and Bo and Charley moved to the door. Charley reached cautiously for the latch, then threw it open. He lunged forward, out onto the sheltered porch, Bo right after him. The horseman turned and faced him, then slowly began to grin.

"Well, Marshal, have you come to turn yourself over to us?"

Charley shook his head. His hand slipped to the butt of his gun.

"No, sir. I don't reckon I'm goin' anywhere. And I don't think you are either."

The horseman leaned forward, frowning slightly. "What did you say?"

The gun slipped from Charley's holster. Leveling it on the rider, he spoke with deliberate coolness. "You heard me. Down off that horse. And if I see you move your hand toward your gun I'll blow you away. You understand?"

The rider was incredulous. "You fool—if I don't come back Noah will come in here shootin' no matter what happens. You're puttin' a noose around your own town if you take me!"

Charley gave no answer, only clicking back the hammer of his .44. The rider gaped, then apparently realizing that the marshal was not kidding, began to dismount. As soon as his boots hit the snow he raised his hands. His horse moved away from him, leaving him standing alone in the street, looking rather pitiful and helpless, a sharp contrast to his cockiness of moments before.

"Slip that gun out of your belt and drop it, then step forward two steps," Charley instructed. As the outlaw obeyed, Charley spoke low to Bo.

"We got a new situation now, Bo. That's Farril Royster, one of Noah's oldtime gang members. As long as we've got him we got an ace up our sleeve when it comes down to dealin' with Noah. The old boy made a blunder when he sent him in. I guess he figured we would be too scared to try to take him."

"You sure that's Royster, Charley?"

"Yep—recognized him from wanted posters. We got us a trump card now."

It took Charley by shock when the noise of a gun blast tore open the night. The approaching man jerked and gasped, and pitched forward as if he had been struck from behind with a club. Blood stained the back of his leather jacket, spreading out slowly to drip from his body into the snow. Charley watched with intense shock, and Bo cursed.

"Who in the. . ."

Charley rushed into the street and on past the prone outlaw. He knew he was dead even without checking, for the shot had struck him in the center of his body, knocking him sprawling and no doubt tearing up his insides. Charley was not particularly concerned with Royster, but he wanted whoever fired that shot. Whoever it was, he had knocked out Dry Creek's only chance at gaining an advantage over the Murphy gang.

Charley had seen no flash of fire to give away the location of the gunman, and a quick check with Bo revealed that he had noticed nothing also. Charley looked into windows and checked alleys, but realized that a search would be futile. It wasn't that there were no suspects; it was that there were too many. Every window had at least one face peering out of it; every corner had an onlooker peeping around it. Whoever had fired the shot would not be likely to own up to it, and Charley was too angry, too disgusted to get into a heavy questioning session with the frightened townspeople right now. So with a low curse he turned away and moved back to where the outlaw lay dead in the snow. He nudged the body with his foot. His first instinct had spoken truly. Farril Royster was dead.

"Well, Bo, we've had it for sure now," Charley said. "Havin' Royster here for a hostage was about the only chance we had to maybe settle this without a fight. That chance is gone now. Even if I turned myself in to the Murphy gang it wouldn't make no difference. They'd beat me, torture me until they figured out I really don't know where Willy hid that money, and then they would probably shoot up the town just to show how mad and mean they was. We're in a fix, Bo, and there ain't no way we're gonna get out of it without a fight."

"Who do you reckon shot him, Charley?"

"I got no idea. Could have been Rand doin' it to make things worse, could have been just about anybody else who was just scared and wanted to eliminate one of Murphy's gunmen. Don't really matter, I reckon."

The people started to emerge from the buildings lining the street then. They moved silently toward the dead outlaw and the somber marshal and deputy that stood looking down at him. They gathered in a circle around them, no one speaking, everyone scared and wondering what would come next. All had heard the warning carried by the outlaw, and no one doubted the Murphy gang would do just what they said.

Kathy stood at the rear of the crowd, Rand Cantrell just a few feet from her. She eyed Charley with a cutting, harsh gaze. Then looked to Rand, her mind reeling with the scheme that had been developing since last night.

Sarah emerged from the office and made her way to Charley's side. The marshal slipped his arm around her and drew her close, not concerned with the glances that passed between many of the onlookers as they saw the action. At that moment Charley couldn't have cared less about the opinion of the people. He had sworn to protect them, and had done his best to fulfill that promise, but so far all they had done was the very things that would harm them most. As foolish as sheep they seemed to him then. If it wasn't for folks like Doc and Sarah, this town would hardly be worth defending, or so it seemed to Charley at that moment.

Kathy watched him holding Sarah close, and her face was cold and haughty. When Rand Cantrell headed toward the saloon she moved after him, calling his name softly. He turned, then tipped his hat with his finger and smiled to see the lady approaching.

"Evenin', ma'am. What can I do for you?"

"That isn't the question, Mr. Cantrell. I think once you hear what I have to say you'll agree that it's me that's done something for you."

Cantrell's quick smile flashed again. "That's an intriguing statement, ma'am. Step inside with me and we'll discuss it further."

Kathy balked. The Lodgepole was a man's place, a spot where women of decent raising didn't go. She said as much to Cantrell, and he apologized for what he termed his "indiscretion."

"I'm living in Charley Hanna's old house, where Martha Hanna lived," she said. "Wait until everyone has gone to bed, and slip over a bit past midnight. I have something to discuss with you that you'll find very interesting, if I read you right. You might say we have a common goal, in a way."

"I'll be there, ma'am. You'd be Kathy Denning—am I right?"

"That's right. I'll be waiting."

Kathy turned and moved quickly down the street. Cantrell watched her move away, and smiled after her retreating form. An intriguing and mysterious lady, this

Kathy Denning. He turned and entered the Lodgepole.

And the word began spreading throughout the town of Dry Creek—the suspected attack from the Murphy gang was far more than a suspicion. The little mountain town had two days to prepare itself for a siege.

Chapter 7

After Charley saw to the care of Farril Royster he began
scouring the town, searching not only for some clue
about who might have fired the shot but also trying to
put together some plan for defense.

The town wasn't well-suited to a defense, for it was
bordered by high, rugged hills that would afford plenty
of protection for any sniper that might conceal himself
there. He hoped that when the inevitable attack came
Noah Murphy wouldn't take that approach, for the
people of Dry Creek would be pinned inside their
dwellings, unable to venture into the street or even
return the fire that would rain down upon them. .
Foolish, foolish people, Charley mused. Whoever had
fired the shot that killed Royster had eliminated any
chance for negotiation to hold off a Murphy attack.
Some fool coward, firing from cover in the dark of
night, probably imagining he had done the town a
service.

Charley studied the dark street. As soon as he had
begun his walk about the town the faces in the windows
had vanished, kerosene lamps had winked out, and the
street had become as silent as a grave. He didn't expect
to find the man responsible for Royster's death. Heck,
he thought, maybe it was a woman!

He looked at the southern side of the wide street. On
the end were several residences scattered in an uneven

68

row, with the hardware store close beside them. Then there was the cafe, the gun shop, the livery, the Lodgepole Saloon, and various deserted old buildings. The facing street had another saloon, the Mansfield Saloon, and adjoining it was the Ketchum Boarding House, along with a laundry, the general merchandise store, a feed store, and Gertie Sander's seamstress shop. The church house sat off the main street several yards, on a slight hill. Across from it was another knoll that was dotted with tombstones. It seemed a bit out of balance to realize that in the same ground where his mother lay buried the worthless Willy Murphy also was interred.

Charley paused in the center of the street, looking around him. If the Murphy gang decided to attack the town from the cover of the hills, there would be little to do except wait them out and hope for an occasional shot at them. But somehow Charley suspected they wouldn't fight so covertly. Most likely they would ride into the main street, burning and shooting, doing their best to kill and terrorize. From what he knew of the Murphy gang, that seemed like more their style.

And if they did attack so openly, Charley wanted to have the townspeople in the safest fighting position possible, someplace where they could have a good range of fire into the streets without being exposed themselves.

But that was assuming the townsfolk would go along with Charley in fighting the Murphy gang at all. Right now the marshal wasn't sure just where he stood in the eyes of the people, now that Rand Cantrell had done what he had.

Apparently there were quite a few townspeople who actually suspected Charley of being in league with the Murphys in some way, or at least of killing Willy Murphy after digging out of him the whereabouts of the money. And even those who still believed in his honesty seemed to think that he had been negligent about warning the town of the danger it was in, waiting too long to make the information public.

Maybe he had. But the sudden death of Martha Hanna had been a crushing blow to him, and somehow he hadn't been able to break through the shock of it and voice the warning. And anyway, he had been on the verge of speaking when Rand Cantrell had made his unexpected pronouncement.

Rand Cantrell. That was some character. Charley had hardly given the man a moment's thought until this sorry affair had started. But now he mused about the man and his vindictive action, and felt certain that Rand would continue to spread his accusations around town.

The only motivation Charley could think of was the beating he had administered the fellow sometime before. But that hardly seemed a justification for dividing a town against itself, especially in such a time of danger. He wondered if Cantrell fully realized the possible results of what he was doing.

Charley's thoughts drifted back to the defense of the town. He put his hands on his hips and looked around him.

There was a row of second-story windows above the Mansfield Saloon and the boarding house. From those windows a man could have a good sweep of most of the street below while still being hidden behind thick walls himself. From that vantage point a group might make an able defense for quite a long time.

Charley huddled under the warm thickness of his leather coat and moved back toward the jailhouse. He procured his tobacco bag from his pocket and slipped off his gloves long enough to roll a cigarette. Striking the match on the porch column, he lit the tobacco and thought over his situation.

He could see why some folks who didn't know him

well might suspect him of having greedy intentions toward that Murphy money. After all, many of those folks were greedy themselves, and even now were spending the night in the cold forest rather than their homes because they wanted so badly to find that stolen cash. What a pack of fools they were, unwilling to stay home and build a defense against the coming attack simply because of the intensely remote possibility of gaining easy wealth.

There was a bitter irony in the fact that Charley was trying to protect the same people who were whispering about him behind his back. But he wouldn't let their personal feelings toward him affect the way he did his job. There were people in this town worth protecting—people like Doc and Sarah, among others—and he would stand up to the Murphy gang alone if it became necessary.

He felt he would be willing to stand up to the devil himself if it was Sarah he was protecting. Strange, the way he was beginning to feel about her. In the past she had been just another woman to him, but now. . .

Funny that such a thing should happen at such a difficult time as this. Just when he suspected that he was falling in love he was being forced to put his life on the line. And if Rand Cantrell's crusade against him kept going, there might not be more than a handful of folks willing to fight alongside him.

He looked over at the Lodgepole Saloon, still lit up and running in spite of the late hour. It was a place that never seemed to close its doors—except on Sundays, of course. And then only because the local law required it.

Charley strode across the dark street toward the log building. He figured Rand Cantrell would probably be there, at his usual place at the gambling table or perhaps leaned up against the bar. And he felt a sudden urge to have a talk with the gambler who he felt was largely

71

responsible for this situation.

When he entered he immediately felt the icy stares that greeted him. Even without being told he knew that Cantrell hadn't limited his talking to the funeral.

He looked around the room until he saw Rand Cantrell, leaned against the bar with a shot of red whiskey in his hand. He was talking to some of the local men, who stood beside him at the bar, apparently very interested in what the gambler was saying. Charley could guess just who it was they were talking about.

Cantrell noticed Charley approaching him across the room, and for a brief second there flashed across his handsome face a smile that Charley found strangely irritating. He had the sensation of being a child being teased, some sort of puppet being manipulated by the gambler for the sheer pleasure of watching him dance.

"Hello, Marshal. Funny you should come in—we were just talking about you."

"I'll bet you were. And I'll bet you had plenty to say, didn't you, Rand?"

The gambler took a sip of his drink, dark eyes sparkling above the glass. "What's wrong, Charley? You sound a bit defensive."

"What's wrong is that this town is going to be under siege before long and all of you are sittin' here drinkin' and shootin' bull instead of doin' anything about it. We've got to stop Noah Murphy from takin' this town, and believe me, he's capable of doin' it."

"Know a lot about Noah Murphy, do you?"

Charley's temper flared at the cool, pregnant comment. But he swallowed down his anger and managed to keep a calm air about him.

"I know a little. What are you gettin' at, Rand?"

The gambler glanced around him. Deliberately putting on the countenance of a man doing a painful duty, he looked down at the amber liquid in his shot

72

glass and spoke in a low, smooth voice.

"Well, Charley, I reckon I'm getting at the same thing I talked about at your mother's burial. It seems mighty funny that Noah Murphy wants you so bad. Why is that?"

"Is that so hard to understand? He wants me because he thinks I know where that money is."

"Do you?"

"I answered that question today. No, I got no idea where it is. Willy Murphy died without tellin'."

"Don't take offense, Charley—but how do we know that's true?"

Charley was having trouble controlling his temper now. He wasn't sure how much longer he could restrain himself in the presence of the arrogant, rumor-mongering gambler.

"If I knew where that money was, and if I was as dishonest a fellow as you seem to think, then I wouldn't be hangin' around here, would I? If I had that money and was plannin' on keepin' it myself, I'd be long gone by now, instead of standin' here arguin' with you," Charley exploded.

The gambler never lost his air of calm. Casually he took another sip from his drink, rolling the remnant of the liquor around in his glass and watching the swirling patterns it made. Then he looked up at Charley.

"I've been thinking, Charley, trying to figure your motives out in all of this. And I think I understand why it is you're still around here. Now I'll confess I can't prove that you know where that money is, but look at the facts. First you come riding in with the body of Willy Murphy, saying his brother shot him. Maybe he did, maybe not. It could have as easily been you. Now just after you come in, you have a good chance to warn the town about this danger we're in—you know as well as me that half the population was gathered there staring at those bodies—but still you say nothing. Your deputy overhears you talking to the Doctor and Miss Redding about hidden money. Then the next day at the funeral of your mother you tell the town about the threat of Noah Murphy only after I first bring up what Bo Myers told me. It makes a sensible man suspect that if I hadn't spoken up you would have said nothing about it at all.

"Now there seems to me to be a logical explanation about just why you wouldn't be out in the mountains getting that money right now. Maybe you were telling the truth when you said Noah Murphy shot his brother, and we know that he is still roaming the mountains. We know that he would like to get his hands on you now that that rider came through shouting it to the town. Maybe the reason you're still here is that you're afraid to go out and claim that money while he's still in the area. Maybe you want him to come raiding this town in the hope that he'll get himself killed and you can be free to take that cash. That's what I've been discussing with the men here, and let me tell you, there's a lot besides me that wonder about this. A lot more."

And Charley knew from the looks he was receiving that in his last statement at least Cantrell spoke the truth. The gambler was a convincing man, and his lies had taken seed in the suspicious minds of many of the population of Dry Creek. And the frustrating part of it all was that there was nothing Charley could do to vindicate himself.

"Cantrell, you're a liar and a scoundrel, and any man that listens to you is a fool, but I ain't gonna stand here and argue any more. No matter what you think about me, the fact still remains that everyone in this town is facin' a pretty horrible death if we don't band together to hold out against Noah Murphy. I'd like to thrash you right now, just like I did a while back, but I'll admit I need your gun and your support too much for that right now. We'll take care of our problems after all of this is over. Are you gonna stand with me or not?"

Cantrell drained the last of his drink. "I don't see that we're dependent on you for our defense, Marshal. And we haven't been sitting by and waiting for Noah Murphy to come, either. We have our own plans for defense, and quite frankly we don't feel you are quite trustworthy enough to be in charge. So it looks like I'll be coordinating this defense, should Noah Murphy truly be rash enough to attack the town." He smiled at Charley, who stood clenching his fists and imagining how good it would feel to smash the smug gambler's nose.

"Stick with me, Rand. It will be better if we're all fighting together."

"Sorry, Marshal. The decision is made. Now if you don't mind, I'll take my leave. I've got a card game over there just waiting. . ."

There came the sound of a loud, high-pitched scream echoing down the street. And the voice that made the cry immediately drew Charley's full attention, filling him with a sudden dread.

"Sarah!"

He bolted for the door, forgetting all about Rand Cantrell and his treachery, caring only about finding Sarah. He was hardly out the door before the scream came again. Others in the saloon followed him.

He paused on the boardwalk and looked wildly around, drawing his pistol. There came the muffled sound of Sarah's voice, and Charley's eyes were drawn to a movement in an alleyway down toward the end of the opposite street.

Without hesitation he moved, pounding across the snow-covered street toward the commotion.

Sarah was struggling in the arms of men Charley at

first couldn't recognize. Then a face turned toward him, and he stopped, shocked at what he saw.

William Branton and Max Franklin, two of the town's better-known merchants, stared at him with sudden guilt, mixed with a good dose of fear. Franklin had a scratch down the left side of his face, Sarah's fingernails having created the wound.

"Stop! Let her go!"

Franklin glanced at Branton, apparently unwilling to obey the order. Charley gritted his teeth, raised the pistol in his right hand, and deliberately clicked back the hammer.

"I'll blow your head off, both of you, if you don't let her go *now*."

Branton was pale, and Franklin's eyes looked suddenly like those of a cornered deer about to be shot. The pair took their hands from Sarah as if she were made of red-hot iron, and the disheveled, weeping young woman ran straight for Charley, wrapping her arms around his waist. Charley continued staring at the two men, not lowering the pistol.

Branton managed to choke out a feeble plea. "Charley—what are you aimin' to do? We let her go like you said."

Charley addressed Sarah without taking his eyes off the men. "What were they up to, Sarah?"

"They. . .they wanted me to take them to where the money was," she said. "They said they'd beat me if I didn't tell them."

Charley's lip began to tremble in rage, and slowly he shook his head. "Branton, Franklin—is that true?"

Franklin grinned weakly, putting forth his hands to placate the angry lawman. "Charley, we didn't mean no harm—we was just funnin' with her a little."

The muzzle of Charley's pistol dropped slightly, and the night was filled with the roar of the shot and the echoing cry of Franklin. Then the pistol roared again, two more times.

When the powdersmoke faded the stunned crowd gathered behind Charley saw the two men standing with their faces hidden in their arms, their bodies quaking as if they were frightened children. Only after a full ten seconds did Franklin dare look around again, and Branton waited even longer.

The bullets had entered the ground inches from the feet of the two men, kicking up the ground around their boots. Charley once more clicked back the hammer of his pistol.

"The next shots will be in your guts unless you have your tails outta my sight in five seconds. *Move!*"

The men took off at a dead run, Branton whimpering audibly as he pushed his way through the stunned crowd. Into the alley beside the Lodgepole they ran, disappearing into the darkness, running back to wives that would scold them for not finding out where the money was.

Only after they were gone did Charley holster his gun once more. And he looked sternly around at the crowd.

"If anyone of you ever lays hands on Sarah again—or the Doc, or me for that matter—tryin' to find out where that money is, that man will find his brains splattered across the street. That's a promise."

He put his burly arm around the trembling young woman at his side and walked back toward the jailhouse, leaving the crowd to stare silently after him.

Rand Cantrell moved to the front of the crowd and gestured toward the jailhouse that Charley and Sarah had just entered.

"See that, folks? He's willing to threaten the lives of all of us just to protect his little group of friends. He doesn't care about the welfare of you, me, or anyone else—just so his friends are protected and the secret of that hidden money doesn't get out. Is that the man you want protecting this town against Noah Murphy? Is it?"

There was a mumbling among the crowd, murmured voices of dissent that raised into a tumult. Rand Cantrell waved down the shouts, then looked over the group with a dramatic pause.

"Back there in the saloon a few minutes ago some of the men did me the honor of asking me to head up this town's defense against the Murphy gang. I'm willing to accept if you will give me the word saying that you're behind me. Do I have your support?"

There came an even louder cry of affirmation. Rand bowed and nodded like a politician on election day, and the crowd gathered around him, hustling him back toward the Lodgepole Saloon. From his office overlooking the street Doc Hopkins watched the procession, and his face was weary and sad. Letting the curtain drop from his wrinkled fingers he moved back into the mustiness of his office.

The revelry continued for some time, and at midnight Cantrell slipped out the door and headed on down the street toward the Hanna house, where Kathy Denning awaited him.

Chapter 8

When the sun rose over the snowy peaks the following morning it cast its glow onto a band of sleeping citizens of Dry Creek, who lay shivering and cold beside a scarcely flickering fire, their only shelter a crude lean-to covered with bark and their only protection from the cold their thick clothing and the heaps of heavy woolen blankets on top of them. They had moved from their homes into the snowy wilderness too quickly to make better provision for themselves.

But the little band led by Abel Filson and Martin Arlo had been forced to move quickly, or so they felt, for others had gone into the forests ahead of them in search of the money hidden there by Willy Murphy. Not one of them had a single clue about where to search, but no one was willing to put aside the absurd hunt, for it was just possible, just remotely, deliciously possible, that by sheer chance they might stumble upon it.

Filson and Arlo had led their little group of treasure-seekers to the area nearby Sarah Redding's farm, for that had been where Willy Murphy had died. If it was true that he had been shot by his brother sometime before that, then surely the shooting had occurred not far from the farm, for it didn't seem likely that he would have traveled far with a bullet in him. And if he was shot near the farm, then maybe he had buried the money near the farm, too.

Or so reasoned these money-hungry people of Dry

Creek, people who two days ago were God-fearing churchgoers who would have scoffed at the idea they would ever pursue stolen money with full intention of keeping it for themselves. But two days ago such a prospect would have been laughable, a fantasy with no connection to their mundane, weary world.

Now that the prospect was a real one, things looked suddenly different to the usually moral folks, and a kind of fever manipulated them almost as if they were puppets. Now the same Abel Filson and Martin Arlo who sat on the front deacon's pew on Sunday mornings in Dry Creek's only church were perfectly willing to divide money among themselves that had been taken from a Denver bank.

Arlo shook himself awake as the sun burned down on his face, and it took him a long moment to piece together the situation and figure out just why he was laying on the cold earth rather than in his warm feather bed back in town. Sitting up, he rubbed his head and yawned, the cold morning air slicing painfully into his lungs. Every joint in his body ached from the stiffening effect of the cold and the hardness of the ground.

Filson stirred awake beside him and rose up bleary-eyed and confused. Seeing Arlo, he grunted a sullen greeting and shook his head like a dog flinging water off its ears.

"Lord, that's hard ground. . .awful hard ground," he muttered. The others were waking up now, grumbling and cold. All told, there were five in the party. They had come together under the agreement that the money would be split evenly between them if one of them found it. But in his heart every man in the group was completely ready to keep the full amount for himself if he was the one lucky enough to run across it.

Filson rubbed a face covered with scruffy beard and muttered. The men rose slowly, each gathering his blankets, one of them tossing a few branches onto the dying fire, the icy fragments of snow on them making a sizzling sound as they touched the red coals buried beneath the fluffy heap of ash at the base of the fire.

"Where we gonna look today?" asked Filson after the fire was built up again.

Arlo was filling a tin coffeepot with snow in preparation for making coffee. He shrugged. "I don't know. Maybe we should go to Sarah Redding's house and start around there."

One of the men in the party sat on a fallen log, pulling on his boots. "Do you think Charley Hanna knows where that money is?" he asked. "Rumor has it that him and the Doc and Sarah Reddin' are in cahoots about it."

Arlo laughed. "No, I don't think ol' Charley knows, I really don't. If he did he wouldn't be here. He'd be off livin' it up in Denver or someplace. No, I reckon it happened pretty much like he told it. But that means that money really is out here somewhere, just waitin' for somebody to find it. And I hope that's us."

Filson looked skeptical. "I don't know, Martin. Maybe Charley knows more than he lets on. Maybe he's already got that money."

"If he does, then why is he hangin' around town?" asked Arlo. "No. I reckon that money's out here."

One of the others pulled out an iron skillet and set it on the rocks just to the side of the fire, shoving some of the burning wood beneath it with a stick. "Do you think Noah Murphy will try to get Charley or the other two?"

"No, and I don't think he'd come in against a whole town, neither. He'd be mighty stupid to try somethin' like that—he'd be blown outta this world mighty quick that way. I think ol' Charley just said that to keep us in town so he could go out and hunt for that money himself. But I ain't fallin' for it. Not for a minute."

81

The men fried several hunks of greasy bacon and thawed out a few thick slices of bread above the flames. The aroma caught in the crisp morning breeze and wafted through the forest, tantalizing the men who had the kind of hunger a night spent outdoors always brings. When the coffee began to boil, tin plates and pewter forks and spoons were distributed, and the group sat down to a simple but satisfying breakfast.

Immediately afterward they began their search. It was at first a disorganized affair, until Arlo again voiced his feeling that the search could most logically be made beginning at Sarah Redding's house. The others agreed, some almost reluctantly, for so gripped were they with the fever for easy money that they hated to take the extra time a more systematic search might entail.

The men rode toward the Redding house in an attitude akin to nervousness, and they looked around them as they traveled. They sought not only some sign that might lead them to the money—a hidden footprint, a dark, obscured trail—they also kept on the lookout for the others from Dry Creek that were in the mountains making their own search. . .and for Noah Murphy, a threat they were unwilling to acknowledge openly but which hung in the back of their minds like a stubborn bad memory.

The trail on which they rode was a snow-dusted trail, a trail that led beneath spruces that reached down with evergreen branches to swipe at their heads, as well as pale-barked aspens that were now stripped of their leaves and laden with frost. Through the bare patches in the timber they could see the sky, fairly clear this morning but still holding dark and threatening clouds on the far horizons, and silver-white mountains which loomed majestic and rocky above the timberline that skirted around the barren peaks.

But few in the group took the time to view the scene,

for their eyes were on the earth and the trail before them. When Arlo pulled up to a stop within a few hundred yards of the Redding house, the others stopped behind him. The lead rider bent over and studied the snow on the ground beside his horse's hooves.

"What is it, Martin?"

"Tracks. . .a bunch of 'em. Leadin' toward the Redding house."

"Yeah—I see. I wonder who?"

"Some of the others, I'll betcha," growled one of the men in the rear. "Beat us to it, it looks like."

"Probably. But let's approach the house slow and careful, and be ready to run if it comes to that."

The men started forward again, Arlo no longer looking at the trail but instead scanning the dark woodland around him. He ducked a drooping aspen branch and goaded his horse over a rocky crest in the trail, and entered an area where the pathway circled amidst an outcropping conglomeration of boulders backed by snow-lined scrub brush and a few cedars.

Circling through the rocks, Arlo came out onto the road that led toward the Redding house. He rode as far as he could witout exposing himself to view from the house, then stopped. Filson pulled up beside him, and the others paused behind.

"What are you thinkin', Martin?"

"I don't know. . .those tracks appeared fairly fresh, just a little new snow in 'em. I reckon it was probably some of the others lookin' for the money, but then. . ."

"What are we waitin' on?" said one of the men behind. "Let's ride on and see if there's any sign around the house."

"Be patient, Fred. We gotta be careful about this."

"Careful you say? While we sit here bein' careful, some of the others are over at the house pickin' up sign of that money. I say let's go have a look ourselves."

83

The speaker was Fred Gearhart, a rather stocky, square-jawed man with closely cropped hair and a sour disposition. He had joined the searching party rather reluctantly, wishing to look on his own, convinced to band himself with the others only when someone pointed out the threat of Noah Murphy's presence in the mountains. But even then he had seemed uncertain of his commitment to the group, and appeared ready to take off on his own at the slightest provocation. And his disgruntled spirit had spread to some of the others in the party, as well.

"Doggone it, Fred, we'll take a look. But just slow down here and think about it. Do you want to ride up on that house if Noah Murphy and his boys have been around here recently? Maybe that's just where they are—Sarah bein' in town and all, there ain't nobody there to keep 'em out."

Gearhart's forehead crinkled into a meaty expanse of wrinkles, and his jaws drooped like the jowls of a boxer dog. His heavy brown eyebrows tilted upwards in the center, and he looked like the very image of exasperation.

"If Noah Murphy's around here then we've had it for sure," he said. "I'll grant you that. But how in the devil are we supposed to find out unless we ride in? If we worry about him bein' there, then we ain't gonna move all day. And that ain't no way to find hidden money. I figure that's worth a little risk—if I didn't I wouldn't be out here. If you want to sit here and worry about Noah Murphy, then you can. Buy I'm ridin' in there. Anybody with me?"

The beefy-faced man turned to those alongside of him. For a moment there were uncertain expressions, hesitations. But a thin man in a brown, water-spotted hat twisted his mouth beneath a jungle of drooping mustache and said, "I'll go, Fred. I reckon we won't find no money sitin' here."

The other man bringing up the rear seemed bolstered by the decision of the other and quickly expressed his agreement. Arlo felt a growing sense of uneasiness, as if perhaps he began to realize what a fever of irrationality was manipulating the money-hungry men. He turned an appealing eye to Filson, who looked almost ashamed as he said, "I reckon I'll go with 'em, Martin. The more of us there is the better it would be. There probably ain't nobody at that house, no way."

Gearhart dug his heels into his chestnut mare's flanks and pulled out into the lead. Rounding the concealing bend, he rode bravely toward the house, not even bothering to loosen his pistol in his holster. The others followed, Filson coming up in the rear.

Arlo hesitated, pursing his lip. Though he knew he had been outvoted, something was telling him to not round the bend after the others, warning him. . .

There came the roar of a high-powered rifle piercing through the morning stillness, followed by a horrible, almost inhuman cry, then more shots. Arlo's hand tensed around the saddlehorn, and he listened in horrified shock as the clearing around the bend became a tumult of whinnying, rearing horses, yelling men, and roaring guns.

"Abel! Abel!" Martin Arlo cried out, sudden worry for his friend's life gripping him. He fought off the impulse to dash into the clearing, his hands gripping the saddlehorn in the tension of fear, his face growing pale.

He heard the sound of a rider coming back from the clearing, then another. Filson rounded the bend at a dead run, screaming at the numbed Arlo to follow. There was terror in the rider's voice. Only one other man followed him—the fleshy, gasping Gearhart.

Arlo goaded his horse forward, following after the others, running as if a demon was fast in pursuit. And he guessed that if Noah Murphy and his boys were after them, a demon might be a more preferable pursuer.

Filson and Gearhart were sticking to the main road, heading in the direction of Dry Creek. Martin Arlo almost followed them, but the sound of riders behind him spurred a sudden decision in his mind, and he cut into the dark woodland trail from which they had emerged minutes before, ignoring the slapping, cutting branches that whipped about his face.

Only a short distance off the road he entered the rocky area and pulled his horse to a stop. Dismounting with clumsy haste, he grasped the reins and led the animal around behind the largest of the rocks, his mouth dry, his lips breathing a silent prayer of desperation.

Then came a silence as sudden as the outbreak of shots moments before, and Arlo was conscious of the loud beating of his heart. His horse gave a low whinny, and he desperately tried to quiet the animal.

For a long time there was only silence, then there came the sound of horses moving back up the road on the other side of the trees. This time they were not running.

"That's far enough," said a gruff voice. "Get down."

"Please. . .what are you goin' to. . ."

"Shut up, fatty. Get down. You too, buddy."

Arlo closed his eyes, and horror of it all almost made him vomit. Whoever it was had Gearhart and Filson. And who could it be but the Murphy gang?

"What are you doin' out here?"

"We came. . .we came lookin' for. . ."

Arlo recognized Gearhart's voice, and from the words and tone it was clear that he was grasping for some explanation—any explanation—other than the real one. And he was having no luck.

"Spit it out, fat man. What are you doin' out here? And why did you ride up on the house like you did?"

"We. . .we know the person who lives there, and we came to visit. . ."

There was sudden, cold laughter. Arlo hugged the white rocks and bit his lip, trembling from more than the cold.

"You're a liar. You're a damn liar, and we ain't got time to fool with you. Turn around."

"What? No! Please. . ."

"Turn around. You ain't gonna want to see what I'm about to do."

"No. Lord, please help us. . ."

"Suit yourself, then."

Arlo's body jerked with each jolting roar of the pistol that cleared its throat out on the road not fifty feet away from him. He bit his lip until it bled, suddenly sickened to realize that his best friend who this morning had eaten breakfast with him now lay massacred on the snowy road, killed by the Murphy gang—probably Noah Murphy himself.

"What do you reckon they were doin', Noah?" The question which carried through the trees confirmed the suspicion in Arlo's mind.

"I don't know. Lookin' for us, I reckon. It don't matter. That's just four less to worry about when it comes time to ride into town. I don't figure that marshal plans to turn himself or his friends over to us. And I'm inclined to burn the town even if he does. Go through their pockets and see if they got anything worth keepin'. I'll get the ones in the clearin' over here."

Arlo slid down to a seated position on the earth behind the white rocks that had saved him from detection. Try as he would he couldn't stop trembling. His horse shuffled quietly in the snow, looking down at its master as if confused by his strange posture.

Chapter 9

When Martin Arlo rode into Dry Creek, he received many stares and heard many whispers. Everyone knew that he had been among the number that rode out into the mountains in search of the hidden money, and now that he was returning—alone—the curiosity of the townspeople was being aroused. And when he rode without stopping straight to the door of the marshal's office, there was much murmuring among the people.

He found Charley finishing his morning coffee. Arlo was too distraught to notice the lines of worry and tension that lined the marshal's eyes.

"Hello, Martin. What brings you back?"

The man looked frightened, as if he had looked the very embodiment of death straight in the face. He looked around him, as if he feared listeners hidden in the very walls.

"It was a massacre, Charley, a massacre." He spit the words out in a tense whisper, and Charley felt a sudden cold shiver run through his body.

"Who, Martin?"

The man sank down into the chair beside the oaken table that sat against the side wall. "All of them, Charley, all of them. I'm the only one that got away."

"Just who are you talkin' about, Martin? Was it some of our folks?"

The pale and shaken man nodded. "Yes—hardly an

hour ago. Filson and Gearhart and Paul and Zeke Stone. It was Noah Murphy and his boys that killed 'em. Abel and Gearhart were murdered in cold blood, shot right in the head after they were caught.''

"My God.'' The words had a flat, dull tone to them. Somehow the news did not shock Charley greatly; the way things had been going, he was accustomed to bad news.

"You sure it was Murphy?''

"Yes. I heard 'em talkin' after they killed them. I was hiding in the rocks just off the road that leads to Sarah Redding's house. It was there that they killed 'em.''

Charley strode over to the window and pulled back the curtain. He stared across the sunlit street in a kind of daze. "That means Murphy definitely wasn't bluffing. We've got until tomorrow night, accordin' to what the rider they sent in said. I just hope they hold off that long.''

"Charley, you got my support in anything we can do to defend ourselves against 'em. I was a fool to go off into the woods like that—all of us were. And I'll fight to the death if need be to make up for that mistake.''

Charley turned and looked with appreciation at Martin Arlo. Even as simple a word of support as he had just given seemed to be a tremendous boost just now.

"Thanks, Martin. We'll sure be needin' the help of every man.''

"How do things stand as far as defense goes, Charley? Do you have a plan?''

"The town is divided, Martin. Rand Cantrell has been spreadin' his stories about me, makin' it look like me and Sarah and the Doc were all in league together, tryin' to keep the whereabouts of the Murphy money secret so we could go get it and split it up later. The fact is that none of us know where that money is, but the more I say that the more folks don't believe me.

"They've even started tryin' to beat the information out of us. Last night Branton and Franklin tried to get it out of Sarah. I got her at the Widow Thompkins's place right now, with Bo guardin' the door. And folks are refusin' to cooperate with me in plannin' a defense. They're turnin' to Cantrell as their leader, and he's playin' it for all it's worth.

"I can't rightly figure out why he's so dead set to stir up trouble. I know the man don't like me, but I think it's gone beyond that now. I think he really likes the attention, havin' folks follow after him and all."

Martin Arlo shook his head. "That's bad news. This town needs to be unified if we're gonna stand up to the Murphy boys. They're cold-blooded, Marshal. I know that first hand now."

"So will this whole town pretty soon, Martin. I just wonder if Rand Cantrell is as capable of leadin' the people as he lets on. I just wonder."

Arlo stood up, fingering his hat. "Charley, I don't know if it would be worth tryin' or not—but maybe if you tried to gather the people together and explain the situation we could get things back to normal. Maybe when they hear what happened this mornin' they'll realize how serious all of this really is."

Charley shrugged. "It's worth a try, I reckon. Martin, I'm deputizin' you here and now. You go out and spread the word that I'll meet anybody and everybody in the churchyard at ten o'clock. Right now I gotta go talk to some widows that don't know they're widows just yet."

The lawman pulled on his hat and stepped outside. Martin Arlo watched him leave, then slipped over to the cabinet where Charley kept his whiskey. Pouring himself a stout drink, he downed it without taking the glass from his lips one time, then shook his head.

"I needed that awful bad," he muttered to himself. Glancing into the shaving mirror hanging above the pitcher and basin in the corner, he said, "C'mon, Deputy. Do your work."

He pulled on his hat and walked out into the sunlight.

The crowds began to converge on the church house before ten o'clock. Rand Cantrell was there, and much attention was focused on him. People who before had loathed the gambler as an immoral parasite of the town now spoke of him with great respect, and men and women who had been friends of Charley Hanna for years talked contemptuously of him.

"He ain't concerned about this town," a man declared to Preacher Bartlett. "He was after that money, and now that Rand Cantrell called his hand he's tryin' to save face. He didn't care that the Murphy boys will overrun this town."

The preacher made a feeble defense of the marshal, whom he had always respected, but his words were faltering and uncertain. With the bad talk about Charley Hanna that was floating around him, he was beginning to wonder if perhaps some of the accusations were true.

Charley climbed to the top of the church house steps and raised his hands. Gradually the crowd quietened, and dozens of hostile gazes focused on the marshal.

"Thank you all for comin' out today. I don't need to waste time tellin' you what the problem is. We're facin' an attack from the Murphy gang tomorrow night, and it's important that we have a defense plan worked out."

"Whose fault is it that the Murphy boys are comin', Charley?" a voice called out from the crowd. A hostile murmuring whispered through the group.

Charley tried to locate the speaker, but could not amidst the jumble of faces. "I reckon it ain't nobody's fault," he said. "The way I see it. . ."

"The way I see it it ain't hard to figure whose fault it is!" came another voice. "Everybody knows!"

Charley felt his temper rising. He did his best to squelch the growing fire of rage within him. Losing his temper could only make things worse.

"Like I was sayin'," he continued, "we gotta work up a defense against the Murphys before tomorrow night. If we don't, they'll ride in here and take us over quicker'n you can imagine. If we all band together. . ."

Rand Cantrell stepped forward. "Excuse me, Marshal," he said. "You're a little behind on your information. We *are* banded together. We have been for quite some time now. And we are making a defense plan already. The way I see it, this meeting is a waste of time."

Charley glared coldly at the man. "It's no waste. This town is divided right now, Rand. We need to work together if this thing is goin' to work. And as the marshal, it seems to me that I should be the one to lead the defense.

"Most of you know that four of our men were killed this morning by the Murphy boys while they were out lookin' for that money. And there are still other search parties out there that might be facin' the same death this very minute. That's the hostile kind of folks we're gonna be fightin' tomorrow night. I have experience at that kind of fightin'—and it should be me that leads this town, not some loud-mouth gambler."

Rand smiled faintly, and the crowd responded to Charley's comment with hoots of derision. Rand raised his hand to quiet them.

"Marshal," he said, "it sems to me that if you were so fired up about saving this town from the Murphys you would do the only manly thing possible—surrender yourself to them like they demand. It's you they want, not this town. It's you that knows where that money is

92

hidden. If you go to them, tell them what they want to know, and fulfill their demands, then this town would be out of danger."

The crowd cheered the suggestion, and Charley's face reddened in further anger. After the noise died down he responded.

"I'm afraid things ain't that simple, Rand," he said. "For one thing, I can't tell 'em where the money is 'cause I don't know. And when they finally figured out that I don't know they'd likely burn this town just for spite. Now that Farril Royster is dead it's almost certain that they'll attack no matter what. And it's my duty to stay here and protect this town as best I can."

The crowd roared its disapproval, and Rand seemed to swell with pride to hear the evidence of the town's support for his harrassment of the marshal. He had never before been able to imagine the sweetness of being viewed with respect. He intended to ride the wave of support just as far as it would take him.

The gambler walked up the steps and stood beside Charley. Smiling at the marshal, he turned and looked almost majestically over the crowd. Charley started to speak, to order him down off the porch, but the gambler beat him to the punch.

"Folks, there is more to this than has yet been told. There is a further reason why Charley Hanna shouldn't be trusted to defend this town against the Murphy gang. He is, after all, their own kin."

There was a sudden, overhwelming silence. Charley was every bit as shocked as the crowd to hear the wild statement. What could Rand Cantrell mean, calling him "kin" of the Murphy gang?

"What are you talkin' about, Rand?" he exploded.

"Maybe Kathy Denning should be the one to explain this," Cantrell said. "Miss Denning, come up here, please."

Charley felt weak. Kathy Denning stood on the edge of the crowd, her face hard and emotionless.

Kathy walked up the steps. Charley looked imploringly at her, but she refused to return the look. She walked up and stood beside the gambler. The crowd was quiet now, prepared to hear an explanation of the unbelievable pronouncement Cantrell had just made, and Charley was so stunned, so confused, that he could say nothing.

"Just tell the folks what you told me last night," Rand said. "Speak up loud so everybody can hear."

Kathy's voice quaked slightly when she began speaking, but she spoke loudly and with determination. Charley suffered under the blow of seeing the lady he had liked and trusted for years so inexplicably turning against him.

"Last night I talked to Mr. Cantrell, giving him information I thought was important," she said. "It wasn't an easy thing for me to do, but under the circumstances I had no choice.

"Charley Hanna has more of a relationship with the Murphy gang than has been told so far. Shortly before she died Martha Hanna left a written message for me explaining that she was a sister to Jack Murphy, the father of the Murphy brothers. And Charley has been aware of that relationship all of his life. One of the things Martha was concerned about was Charley's interest in his cousins' activities. She wrote that he had talked many times of getting a share of their money if ever it became possible.

"And because of that I don't think it's advisable to trust Charley Hanna to defend this town. All he wants is to get Noah Murphy out of the way so he can obtain that hidden money. His concern isn't the safety of this town. I recommend that all of you give your support to Mr. Cantrell, and as soon as this situation is through, that the move be made to remove Charley Hanna from his office. Any man that has such a connection with a criminal gang should not serve as marshal of a town.''

The crowd mumbled and shifted, staring at Charley as if he were a freak. And so stunned was the marshal, so overwhelmed at the proclamation Kathy had made, that he simply stood with his mouth hanging open in an expression which many interpreted to be one of guilt.

Rand Cantrell looked haughtily at Charley. ''Can you deny the truth of what was said, Marshal?''

''You're darn right I can! There is not a trace of truth in it. My mother had no connection at all with the Murphy family, and I've never—*never*—made any of the kind of statements like Kathy just said I did. Never! Cantrell, I don't fully understand why you want to spread lies like you are, and Kathy. . .Kathy, of all the people in the world, why would you do this? Why?''

Kathy turned a cold gaze upon him, her lips set firmly in hate. In her eyes was only the faintest hint of remorse. She gazed at Charley only a moment, then descended the stairs.

''Marshal, it looks like the decision has been made,'' said Cantrell. ''The town isn't behind you anymore.''

''Don't speak so fast, Cantrell,'' said Martin Arlo, who had been standing toward the front of the crowd throughout the meeting, looking increasingly angry.

He darted quickly up the stairs and pushed Cantrell aside. ''Listen to me,'' he said. ''I've known Charley Hanna for years, and in all of that time I've never seen him do one thing that would make me doubt his honesty. And if the lot of you were honest, you'd have to admit the same thing. He's a good man, and one who knows his business when it comes to fightin' outlaws like the Murphy gang. He had a good teacher, and that was his pa.

''But Cantrell here is nothin' but a two-bit gambler

who likes to imagine he's a big man. All of you know that he's had it in for Charley ever since Charley thrashed him that night a few months back. He's usin' you people to get back at Charley, that's all. He's not got the experience or the knowledge needed to lead a defense against the Murphy gang. I'm puttin' my money on Charley Hanna. I was foolish enough to take the threat of the Murphy boys lightly one time, but that won't be any more. I know now just what we're up against, and I won't trust my safety to the direction of a two-bit gambler!"

There came a tremendous roar of dissension, but amidst the voices Charley noticed a handful of supportive cries, and the expressions on some of the faces indicated that at least a few people were cheered to hear Martin Arlo speaking up for the marshal.

After the yelling died down once more, Arlo gazed seriously across the crowd. When he again spoke, his voice was lower. "I'm standin' behind Charley Hanna, folks. I believe there are those among you who would like to do the same. Now isn't the time to be cowed by all the yelling and hollerin' Cantrell has been stirrin' up. If you're with me and Charley, then come on up here and stand with us. If this town is goin' to be split up, there might as well be a clear-cut division."

For a moment there was no response, but then movement at the fringes of the crowd indicated that some were accepting the challenge. One by one people began filing up to the church steps, and Cantrell tried to not show his surprise at the number that still were behind Charley. All of the shouting and ruckus of his supporters had made him think he had more support than he truly did.

But when the last man stepped up onto the porch, it was obvious that the majority of townspeople were sticking with Cantrell. There was a group of fifteen with

Join the Western Book Club
and GET 4 FREE* BOOKS NOW!
A $19.96 VALUE!

Yes! I want to subscribe to the Western Book Club.

Please send me my **4 FREE* BOOKS**. I have enclosed $2.00 for shipping/handling. Each month I'll receive the four newest Leisure Western selections to preview for 10 days. If I decide to keep them, I will pay the Special Members Only discounted price of just $3.36 each, a total of $13.44, plus $2.00 shipping/handling ($19.50 US in Canada). This is a **SAVINGS OF AT LEAST $6.00** off the bookstore price. There is no minimum number of books I must buy, and I may cancel the program at any time. In any case, the **4 FREE* BOOKS** are mine to keep.

*In Canada, add $5.00 shipping/handling per order for the first shipment. For all future shipments to Canada, the cost of membership is $16.25 US, which includes shipping and handling. (All payments must be made in US dollars.)

NAME: _____

ADDRESS: _____

CITY: _____ **STATE:** _____

COUNTRY: _____ **ZIP:** _____

TELEPHONE: _____

E-MAIL: _____

SIGNATURE: _____

If under 18, Parent or Guardian must sign. Terms, prices, and conditions subject to change. Subscription subject to acceptance. Dorchester Publishing reserves the right to reject any order or cancel any subscription.

Charley, not including Arlo and Sarah. Cantrell looked at the much larger crowd assembled in front of the church, and his confidence, which had been momentarily set back, swiftly returned.

"Well, you've had your say, Mr. Arlo," he said. "And now you've got your group. If you'll be on your way the rest of us will begin planning on just how we're going to defend this town from the danger the marshal has brought upon it."

"Fine," snapped Charley. "You have your meetin'. I got better things to do."

He left then, followed by those who had declared their allegiance to him. They moved as a group down the street to the vicinity of the jailhouse, and Charley stepped up onto the boardwalk to address them.

"I appreciate your support more than you can know," he said. "I was beginnin' to think that the whole blasted town had gone loco. I reckon we'll be needin' to do some plannin' if this defense is goin' to hold out. I just hope Cantrell's group does as well as they think they will against the Murphy boys. They just don't know what they're facin'. But right now there's somethin' I gotta do. You all meet me back here in an hour, and we'll start some serious talkin'. We ain't got much time—the gang will attack tomorrow. And folks, that's gonna be one bad night for this town, the worst I expect it ever will see."

The little gathering dispersed, and Sarah approached Charley. "Charley, is it true?"

"No, Sarah," he said, anticipating her question. "Those were lies that Kathy was spreadin'. I don't understand what's so turned her against me. I really don't know."

Sarah said nothing, but in her heart she suspected that she knew the answer. She was fully aware from the way that Kathy had looked at Charley throughout these past months that the lady was in love with him. But now the whole town was aware of the budding romance between herself and the marshal, and Kathy was understandably enough burning with jealousy. But to go so far as to spread lies about Charley—that seemed inconceivable.

"Sarah, I gotta go talk with Doc. He's about the smartest man I know, and right now I need his advice. I want you to go with me, all right?"

"Certainly, Charley. I want to be with you."

Together they walked across the street and ascended the stairs to Doc's office. They found him inhaling steam from a kettle bubbling on the stove. It was obvious that his cough had been giving him trouble today. Charley figured that's why the man had missed the town meeting.

"Howdy, Doc. Feelin' bad?"

"A little lung trouble, Charley. Hello, Sarah."

"Doc."

"What brings you here, Charley? I hear Cantrell has been causin' his usual share of trouble."

"More than his share, Doc. He's gone beyond what he said before. Now he's speadin' new lies about me."

Charley sighed. "He said that Ma was a sister to Lead Jack Murphy, that I'm a cousin to the Murphy boys and have tried to get in on their jobs in the past. It's a lie, Doc. All of it is a stinkin' lie, Doc!"

The old man had gone suddenly pale and had dropped roughly into a chair. The sudden weakness evident in him made Charley think he had suffered some kind of physical breakdown. He quickly moved to the doctor's side.

"Doc, you all right?"

"I'm all right. . .but, Charley—"

"Yes?"

"I think I should tell you something, something that I

wanted Martha to tell you herself before she died. Sit down, Charley, and listen close to me.

"Now I know as well as you that half of Cantrell's talk is pure fiction, but not all of it, this time. Charley. . .he was tellin' the truth when he said your ma was a sister to Lead Jack. I know it's true, 'cause I knew 'em both years ago.

"It's true, Charley. The man you'll be fightin' tomorrow night is your own cousin, your own kin!"

Chapter 10

Charley's expression didn't change for a moment; he stared blankly at the old doctor as if he didn't comprehend what he had said. And then his face twisted into a frown as he considered what the Doc had told him.

"Doc, are you kiddin' me? You mean Kathy was telling the truth?"

"At least about you bein' kin to the Murphy boys, she was. I'm sorry you had to find out at a time like this, Charley. Let me tell you all about it."

"I wish you would. I can't believe. . ."

"Charley, I knew your mother years ago, when both of us lived in Denver. That was before she ever met your Pa, and I wasn't even practicin' medicine at the time. I was a pretty rough fellow, I'll confess, and I rubbed shoulders with a lot of the scum of this earth—includin' Lead Jack Murphy. He was in Denver at the time, and the first time I saw him he was sittin' at a cafe table with his sister—your mother, Charley.

"I don't recall just how it was that I met your mother, but Denver was a lot smaller town in those days. We got to be pretty good friends, and she confided in me about a lot of things, includin' how she worried about how her brother seemed to be gettin' into things he shouldn't. The first bank Jack ever robbed was right there in Denver.

"His name got to be known pretty fast, and people got to callin' him Lead Jack because of how much ammunition he kept strapped in a belt around his waist. And as his reputation grew, the more ashamed Martha got to be.

"She moved away from Denver not long after Lead Jack killed his first man, and she changed her name to Simmons. That's what she went by when she met your Pa, and she never told him different. I didn't ever know what happened to her until I came to Dry Creek. When I saw her it brought back a lot of old memories, let me tell you! We talked, and I promised her I would never let her secret out. And until now I haven't.

"When all this trouble with the Murphy boys came up, I told Martha she ought to tell you about it. If a man is going to fight his own kin he has a right to know that's who they are. But Martha died before she ever told you."

"Kathy said she found a written message."

The old man nodded. "So that's it. She was probably writing that message to you, Charley. That was her way of tellin' you. But Kathy must have found it first."

Charley whistled. "Lord have mercy, what a thing to find out! Before I would have busted the head of any man who tried to link me up with the Murphy boys. I like to have busted Rand Cantrell's head today. I never would have thought about a thing like this."

Sarah interrupted rather hesitantly. "But Charley, she still was lying when she said you had talked about getting involved with the gang and all. She talked like you knew all along you were kin to them and wanted to take advantage of it."

"Yea, I reckon she did lie. And I can't understand that, either. Kathy has always been close to the family, a real good friend. Ma loved her like a daughter."

"Folks do strange things when they're in danger,"

101

said Doc. "You can't always predict what somebody will pull."

"Now I've got another problem," Charley sighed. "I told the whole town that I have no connection with the Murphys. Am I supposed to head right back out and deny it? Rand will sure use that against me. It would sound like I was a born liar—sayin' one thing one time and the opposite the next minute."

Doc shrugged. "I don't reckon it matters, Charley. Those that don't like you will believe what Rand says no matter what, and those that believe in you likely will stick with you to the end whether you tell 'em about this or not. So why say anything at all? Just let it go. I can't see that it will help this town for you to admit any kind of mistake at the moment. And your job is to help it as best you can."

Charley pondered Doc's words. Twisting his lip, he shrugged. "That makes sense, Doc. I reckon we might as well keep it our secret until this mess is finished. So as far as this town is concerned, I'm still denyin' any family connection with the Murphy gang. I'm still calling Rand Cantrell a liar."

Charley and Sarah went back down into the street shortly before the planned gathering to set up a defense was ready to begin. Charley once again studied the windows on the second stories of the boarding house and the Mansfield Saloon.

"If we had gunmen up there they would have a wide sweep of the street," Charley pointed out to Sarah. "And if we had the street barricaded, then we could keep the Murphys from getting in close enough to set fires. And if they circle and come in from the other side, those in the windows can cover that end. We can barricade that side, too, if Rand is willin' to cooperate."

The meeting took place. The meager handful of men

still loyal to the marshal looked pitifully small gathered on the porch of the jail. The marshal looked at the cluster of somber men and shook his head slowly.

"We ain't much of an army, are we? Let's hope Rand does a good job with his fellers. Otherwise we ain't got much more than an even chance of beatin' the Murphys, if that much."

Charley outlined his plan to the group. Using feed bags from the livery, furniture from the stores and houses, wagons, barrels, anything, the street would be barricaded on both ends. Men would be positioned at each barricade, and sharp-eyed riflemen would cover the street from the windows atop the boarding house and Mansfield Saloon. Every other alleyway would be barricaded also, as much as possible, and when the job was done the town would be a makeshift fort.

But it would be a fort with two commanders. And Charley feared that the double command would be what would undo the town if anything would. But he wouldn't give up his authority just for the sake of making things more unified. After all, the protection of Dry Creek was *his* job, not Rand Cantrell's. He had sworn to protect the town when he took the job, and he would do it if it killed him.

Charley answered questions that the men had about the defense, and as a group they walked into the light of the main street and looked it over. The skies had cleared during the previous night, though the cold was still biting, and the street still filled with snow, packed down from the many feet that had walked across it. For once in his life Charley was dissatisfied with Dry Creek's wide streets; narrow ones would have been easier to defend.

Jefferson Novak, town gunsmith, approached Charley. "I got an idea that might help us out," he said.

"What's that?"

"Gunpowder. I got barrels of the stuff, stored out back of the shop. It's buried, most of it. But it's dry—I always make sure of that. Get us some empty bottles from the saloon, a few fuses. . ."

"And we got us some ready-made hand bombs," said Charley, smiling. "Good idea, Jeff."

The marshal followed the lanky gunsmith to his shop, cutting through an alley to round the back of the building.

Novak stopped, looking perplexed. "Well. . .I can't figure that out. It looks like somebody has dug here."

Charley looked at the ground. The dirt had been turned recently, it appeared, then thrown back in place with little effort to smooth it down.

"You didn't do this, Jeff?"

"No. sir. I buried that powder in October and ain't touched it since."

"Get a shovel. We'll check this out."

The two men dug into the soft dirt, quickly displacing it to reveal a trapdoor made of thick pine planks fastened together. Novak tossed his shovel aside and reached for the leather strap that served as a handle to the trapdoor. With a creak and groan the door lifted open to reveal a wood-lined chamber placed into the earth, large enough to hold several sizeable kegs.

But there were no kegs in the chamber. It was empty—the powder obviously stolen. Novak looked incredulously into the empty hole, then turned to stare at Charley.

"Gone. But who could have took it? And why?"

Charley pursed his lips. "There's several who might have taken that powder. Let's hope it wasn't the Murphy gang. If they have that stuff then we're up the creek for certain. But it might not be them. I think we ought to have a talk with Mr. Rand Cantrell about this."

104

Charley turned and strode off with a fast pace toward the Lodgepole. He figured Rand would be there—the place had been like an unofficial headquarters to the man for the many months he had been in Dry Creek.

Novak followed Charley back through the alleyway to the street, then on down toward the log building that housed the Lodgepole Saloon. Charley pushed his way into the building, glaring around the room until he saw Rand Cantrell seated at a corner table, some of his cronies around him.

"Well, hello, Marshal! Didn't expect to see you."

"Shut up, Cantrell. I came to ask you what you know about some gunpowder missin' from Jeff Novak's shop."

Rand Cantrell frowned. "I don't know what you're talking about, Marshal. Are you trying to accuse me of. . ."

"That powder is needed for the defense of this town. If you know anything about it, you'd best start talkin'."

Rand looked at him coldly. "I haven't stolen any gunpowder from Jeff's store, Marshal. Remember, I'm trying to defend this town too. I didn't even know there was any gunpowder stored there."

Charley frowned, feeling exasperated. He realized that even if Cantrell had taken the powder, he would have no way of proving it. And certainly the gambler wasn't about to confess.

"Well, if you didn't take it one of the Murphy boys must have slipped in and dug it out. It wouldn't have been hard to do, and if they were lookin' for powder it would be likely that they would look at a gunsmith's place first."

Cantrell pulled a long cigar from his pocket and lit it. He looked at Charley through the smoke and said, "I reckon it might be a good idea to find out what you have in mind in defending this town, Marshal, since you will

105

insist on leading a defense in spite of the fact that most everyone in the town wants me to do it. If we're both going to do it, we might as well try to not interfere with each other.''

"That's the first smart thing I've ever heard you say, Rand. I reckon it won't hurt to tell you. We're plannin' on barricadin' the streets and alleys, and puttin' riflemen up in the windows of the Ketchum Boarding House and the Mansfield Saloon. We had planned to use that powder for hand bombs, but it looks like that ain't gonna happen.''

Rand nodded slowly. "Sounds logical. We were just siting here trying to figure up our own final plans. We planned to barricade the street, too. I'll have riflemen on top of the Lodgepole and some of the adjacent buildings.''

"You have more riflemen than I do. If we're goin' to try to cooperate on this, then why don't you send some of 'em over to the other side of the street with my boys?''

"No, Marshal. They all stay on this side. All of them.''

Charley frowned. "But why? It would be a lot more effective if—''

"Sorry. I have my reasons. They'll all stay on this side of the street. And I'll be keepin' an eye on you, too. Anybody whose fighting his own kin isn't to be trusted too far. For all I know you might be siding with them.''

Charley felt his throat tighten and his face grow red. Cantrell was pushing him, and it wouldn't take much more before he would push too far.

"You can trust me. I'll do anything I have to to keep this town safe.''

"Anything?''

"You heard me.''

"Then why don't you turn yourself over to the

Murphy gang? You are what they want."

"No, Rand. I've gone through all of this before. You know as well as I do it would do no good. This town is already doomed. When whatever fool it was shot Farril Royster, this town's death warrant was signed. The Murphys will want revenge for that, whether they get their money or not. Sendin' me out there would be nothin' but throwin' away a good gun at a time we need every gun that's available."

Cantrell gave a short, derisive laugh. "So you say, Marshal. Very well, then stay and fight with us. But surely it must bother you to think of all those that might die just because you're not willing to face up to the danger that you yourself brought on this town. After all, it was because of you that Noah Murphy issued his ultimatum."

"Shut up, Cantrell. You're a liar and fool, and I have no time to waste with you. You took on a lot of responsibility when you decided you wanted to be this town's guardian. I just hope you know what you're in for. When you bite off a hunk of the Murphys, you got a tough mouthful to chew."

There came a cry from the street then. Charley recognized the voice of Martin Arlo.

"Charley! Come quick! We got trouble!"

Charley turned and headed for the door, some of the saloon occupants following him. Rand Cantrell looked vaguely disturbed, but he didn't let his thin, smug smile fade for more than an instant.

Charley stepped out onto the boardwalk, looking westward to the end of the street.

Riders came down the street. But they were strange riders, stiff and pale, blood soaking their shirts. Charley recognized them as other men that had gone into the mountains to search for the hidden Murphy money. There were nine of them, all riding in the same stiff fashion, their hands dangling at their sides, some of the faces turned open-mouthed toward the sky. They were dead. All of them. Strapped in their saddles with stout sticks lashed to their backs, holding them grotesquely erect.

Around Charley the occupants of the saloon gathered, their faces as pale as those of the dead riders that made a ghastly parade down the middle of Dry Creek's main street.

Chapter 11

For a time the street settled into a sudden, morbid silence. The sheer, stomach-turning horror of what was happening burned into the mind of every man and woman who stood as an appalled witness to the silent parade of death.

Charley heard the faint, hissing cry of a woman across the street, then saw her collapse to the board-walk. And well she might; her brother was among the dead riders that plodded down the middle of the street. The motion of her fall seemed to jerk the astonished crowd out of its stupor, and immediately loud cries arose from many throats, and people emerged from dark doors, their faces pale and lips trembling. Two of the more stalwart men who had emerged behind Charley from the saloon moved out into the street and caught the lead horses by the reins, pulling them to a stop. The other horses stopped behind them.

"Lord God, have mercy on us."

"My own brother. . .look what they've done to my brother."

The voices were low, almost as if the speakers were in some sacred place. But it was the unbearable horror of it all that muted the voices, the incredible absurdity of the death procession the murderous Murphy gang had arranged for the benefit of the town.

Charley had witnessed many horrible sights in his

day, and he had reached the point that he thought nothing could turn his stomach. But the sight of the dead men strapped into their saddles, their backs stiffened with wooden supports—that made him feel weak, almost faint. Not so much from the sight of death, but from the immense cruelty of the Murphy gang, who not only had killed these men of Dry Creek but also made a public display of their terrible work, almost as if to hint of what was to come for the rest of the town on the following night.

Charley stepped out into the street. "Get 'em down," he ordered. "As quick as you can."

Bo Myers emerged from the jailhouse and walked out into the snowy street with Martin Arlo. Other men joined them, many of them trembling and pale, and quickly the loosened the bonds holding the bodies in the saddles. The stiff corpses slid from the saddles to the earth, their legs still bowed as they had been over the backs of the horses, stiffened by cold and rigor mortis.

Charley looked around him. Almost all of the townsfolk were gathered on each side of the street, standing silently as witnesses to the greatest horror Dry Creek had ever known. And from the expressions on many of the faces Charley could tell that the true danger the town was facing was only being fully realized by many of the townsfolk. Even Rand Cantrell seemed taken aback, his face pale and gaunt.

Almost before he realized it, Charley found himself addressing the people.

"Look at it, folks. This is the work of the Murphy gang. This is the work of the people we'll be facing tomorrow night. They're cruel men, as bad a killers as you'll ever see. They'll put your homes to the torch and murder your children and do things to your wives that you would vomit to think about. And instead of pullin' together and preparing to stop them short of killin' us all, this town has divided and argued over just who is goin' to head up the defense. Well, I'm sayin' the time has come to quit arguing and start gettin' ready for what's comin'. 'Cause what's comin' is going to be nothin' short of hell.''

"And it's goin' to be your kin bringin' it!" a voice shouted from somewhere in the crowd.

Charley turned a stern eye in the direction of the speaker. "I've said I'm not kind to the Murphys in any way, and that ain't changed. And I don't care if Noah Murphy was Preacher Barlett's grandma—he's still gonna be one tough enemy. You want to know why he killed these men instead of takin' them as hostages? Because he wants a fight, that's why! He don't want to avoid it. He's ready to burn a town, and nothin' is going to stop him. Unless it's us.

"Now there's a few of you that's stuck with me. The rest of you seem to think you should trust your safety to the orders of a two-bit gambler. Well, I'm givin' you a chance to change your minds. I've got a plan to fight the Murphys, but I need good men to carry it out. Do I have them?''

Charley could tell his words were having an effect. Men that before had been dead set against the marshal, bound to stay with Rand Cantrell, now looked at each other with doubt in their eyes. And Cantrell could sense he was losing his control over many of his men. The gambler looked nervously at those around him, a disturbed expression on his face.

"It's not gonna pay when things come down to the actual fight for everybody in town to be followin' a different drummer," Charley said. "You can't win a war with two generals contradictin' each other. I'm paid to help this town, to keep it safe, and I'm the only man here with the experience and know-how to do it. Now if you are with me, then come over here and stand beside me. Now."

Hardly had Charley finished speaking before men began to step down from the boardwalk, pushing right past Rand Cantrell to join Charley on the street. It was a handful at first, but then others followed, until when it was over there were more men gathered at Charley's side then Rand Cantrell had left beside him.

Charley smiled faintly. The men Cantrell had left were those whom he had tangled with in the past, men who had reason to hate the marshal. But that was all right with Charley; at least now the sides were clear, and he had a vastly increased team of fighters on his side.

"Good. Real good," Charley said. "Now let's get these bodies out of here and start talkin' about just what we're goin' to do tomorrow night."

Rand Cantrell looked at Charley with an almost murderous expression, then wheeled about and entered the Lodgepole. His greatly reduced band of followers trailed in after him.

Kathy Denning stood in front of the boarding house long after the other women who had been drawn out by the parade of dead riders vanished into the buildings. She watched Charley talking to the men in the street, his arms making sweeping gestures as he described his proposed street and alley barricades. The lady's eyes were brooding and thoughtful. Silently she stepped across the street, heading for the Lodgepole. She had never set foot inside the building before, but this time she felt she had no choice.

She found Rand Cantrell seated at his usual corner table, frowning and thoughtful. His men were scattered around the saloon, away from him, apparently ordered to leave him alone. Kathy walked directly up to him and sat down.

"Mr. Cantrell, I think I need to talk to you. I think we've made a mistake."

112

The gambler glanced harshly at her. "What do you mean?"

"I think it was wrong to lie about Charley Hanna and the Murphy gang."

"What lie? It's true that he's kin to Noah Murphy."

"Don't play games with me. You know what I mean. The lie about him knowing he was kin to them and talking about getting in on their crimes. That was wrong. It should have never been said."

The gambler's angry eyes stabbed into her. "You're sure changing your tune, lady. Not more than a few hours ago you were ready to hang Charley Hanna if you got the chance. Why the change?"

Kathy looked away. "I don't know. . .it just wasn't right to lie."

Cantrell leaned forward, studying her. "Was it right for Charley Hanna to ignore you and take to Sarah Redding like he has?"

Kathy's face grew suddenly red, burning. Cantrell seemed to have looked into her very soul and read her motives and deepest feelings that she thought she had kept secret.

Cantrell smiled. "It's more obvious than you think, Miss Denning. Love is a hard secret to keep."

Kathy lowered her eyes, feeling his stare burning into her. "Ah, I've embarrassed you. My apology. But don't feel ashamed. I think that you of all people should understand why Charley Hanna doesn't deserve to have all the honor that is being heaped on him by that bunch of fools who are ready to trust him with their lives."

"You didn't call them fools when they were following you."

Cantrell ignored the comment. "He jilted you, Miss Denning. Rejected you. Why are you defending him now? Do you think he deserves it?"

Kathy paused, thinking. "No. I guess he doesn't."

"Then you'll keep our little secret?"

The pause was longer this time. But at last Kathy sighed and nodded. "Yes. I won't say anything. I don't know how I could explain why I lied anyway."

Cantrell smiled. "A good decision, Miss Denning. Here's to you." He raised his glass of rye whiskey and took a sip.

Outside in the street Charley was talking seriously to the men gathered around him.

"I have reason to believe the Murphy gang has their hands on a lot of gunpowder," he said. "A good number of barrels turned up missing from the gunsmithy this morning. We had plans to use that powder to make handbombs, but there's no way now. I'm afraid the Murphys have the same idea. If they do, then we're liable to find ourselves scattered in little pieces all over these mountains."

"What are we goin' to do with the women?"

"Kids and old folks and women we'll keep in the back of the boardin' house. The older boys will help load for those in the upstairs here at the saloon and boardin' house. Everybody will have a part to play, just about."

The rest of the day passed with further planning, and by evening the building of the barricades began. Lanterns and torches were brought out into the street to illuminate the work, and even the children were involved in dragging heavy furniture from the saloons and houses, boarding house and other places of business. Several of the huskier men moved to the church house and began dragging the heavy pews out to form the basis of the barricade on the opposite end of the street.

The alleys were filled in with bags of feed from the livery until all of them were used up. Then empty burlap sacks were dug up from somewhere, and several of the town's youths were put to work filling them with dirt and stacking them in the remaining unblocked alleyways. When even those were used up, the remaining alleys were blocked with all the extra furniture that could be found.

By the time the moon was shining clear in the cold night sky high above Dry Creek the town was like a fortress. Every means of access to the central portion of the main street was blocked, and the townspeople were moved within the boundaries of the makeshift fort, most of them crowded into the boarding house. There was much grumbling about being shifted to such uncomfortable quarters a full night before the expected attack was to occur, but Charley was taking no chances. He feared the Murphy gang might make their threat good early so as to catch the town unprepared.

Rand Cantrell gave only reluctant cooperation to Charley Hanna, keeping his handful of men in the Lodgepole, from where he would make his defense, he said. Charley didn't argue with him; the roof of the Lodgepole would make a good vantage point from which to fight. If Cantrell wanted to keep his men there, that was fine with Charley.

The men that Rand Cantrell had left with him were the scum of the town, those that had no love for the law. Joe and Freddy Marcus were among them, along with others a lot worse. When the heat of the battle was on, Charley knew none of Cantrell's men would listen to orders from the marshal they so disliked. He had to admit he had given many of them reason to dislike him; those with no respect for the law had never received any respect from Charley Hanna.

When the defenses were completed Charley gathered the men for a solemn ceremony of straw-drawing. Some would have to fight in the street, behind the barricades, others in the greater safety of the buildings. There had been a handful of volunteers for the outside duty—Charley and Bo among them—but the others decided to leave the decision to chance. When it was done there were ten men in all who would be given the job of fighting behind the makeshift breastworks that spanned the wide street; the others felt fortunate to have been spared the front-line task.

But even the buildings would not be safe, everyone realized. Especially if the Murphys really did have the gunpowder from Novak's gunsmithy.

It was midnight before the town at last settled down to sleep. But few got any rest that night. And those that did found their dreams to be strange and horrible ones, filled with images of death.

Chapter 12

Noah Murphy chewed on the stub of a cigar as he watched his men rolling a keg of gunpowder over to a clearing in the snow outside the Redding cabin. He wanted to light the burned out stub, but he knew that one hot ash striking that gunpowder would blow him and all of his men clean off the mountain.

It had taken a lot of daring to get the powder, right under the nose of the entire town, but Noah had managed to do it. Shifting the cigar stub from one side of his mustached lip to the other, the sandy-haired outlaw watched as his men pryed the lid off the keg, exposing heaps of the grayish powder within the compact keg. Murphy smiled. Dry Creek wouldn't stand a chance now, not while the Murphy gang had this powder.

He had kept a close watch on the town from his post in the mountains the last few days. He knew of the town's fortifications, but they did not worry him. It would take more than a line of wagons, feed sacks, and barrels to stand up to the assault he had planned for the town.

He wasn't certain whether or not Charley Hanna or the other two that had been with Willy before he died had any idea where the money was. It was only a remote possibility that Willy had talked before he died, but Noah Murphy had to assume that he had. Otherwise there would be no hope of ever finding that cash. The men from Dry Creek that had tried had been fools. They were dead fools now. Noah Murphy had enjoyed watching their ghastly parade as it loped through the center of town. If only he could have been close enough to have seen the faces of the townsfolk. He would have enjoyed that very much.

Until all of this had happened Dry Creek had been just another town to Noah Murphy. But now he hated the place and everyone that was in it. Dry Creek had murdered Farril Royster, the only man who Noah Murphy had ever regarded as a friend. And for that crime it would pay.

And besides, Noah always enjoyed burning a town. He hadn't done that in a while.

"We got it open, Noah. Now how are we gonna make those bombs?"

Noah Murphy moved over to where the keg of powder stood, several others beside it. Clamping his teeth down on his cigar butt, he smiled.

"Looks good, looks good. Billy, hand me that empty bottle over yonder."

A young man in a checked shirt scurried to where a discarded whiskey bottle laid up against the side of a stump. He handed it to Murphy.

"Now get me a piece of paper. Tear it out of a book in the house if you have to."

The young man disappeared into Sarah Redding's house and came back with a sheet of paper, a page torn from a Bible. Noah Murphy took it and rolled it into a sort of funnel and inserted the small end into the mouth of the bottle.

"Now we start fillin' the bottle," Murphy said. He reached into the barrel and came up with a heaping handful of powder. Pouring it into the bottle, he repeated the action until the bottle was almost full.

Then he reached to the ground and picked up a stick with a blunt end.

"Now we pack it down," he said, extending the stick into the bottle. He began probing and pounding into the powder, packing it in until it was tightly compressed in the glass.

"Do you have any of those fuses left from the Denver job?" he asked one of his men. The fat, red-headed man grunted and moved over to where a saddle was laid across the top rail of a fence. Digging into one of the saddlebags, he pulled out a long roll of fuse.

"Got more left than I thought," he said.

"Great. It'll come in mighty handy. Cut me off some and stick it down in the bottle."

The man complied. Noah Murphy thrust the end of the fuse deep into the powder, then reached down and began gathering small pebbles, which he dropped into the bottle along with occasional pinches of powder. When the bottle was full, he packed the contents as tightly as he could once more. Then he held up the bottle with a smile.

"And here we have what's gonna blow Dry Creek off the map," he said. "And this here's a small one. We can make 'em a lot bigger and drop a few of those buildings around their ears."

"How are we gonna get through those barricades?"

Noah smiled all the more. "We'll make one of these bombs out of a whole keg of powder, fill it halfway up with rocks or anything we can find. Then we'll roll that thing right up the street. When it blows half the town will go with it. Sound good to you boys?"

"Sounds good. Real good."

"Then let's get to makin' bombs. Come nightfall we got a job to do in Dry Creek."

Every moment that passed only increased the tension

in the air at Dry Creek. It was a town that was waiting. Commerce had stopped; men with rifles in their hands stared with blank eyes at the hills, wondering when the attack would come. The morning sun climbed high and crossed the crest of the heavens, beginning a westward descent that marked the hours until the moment the entire town dreaded.

The women and children, along with the infirm and old, had been sent to the back rooms of the Ketchum Boarding House to wait until it was all over. Though it was still early in the afternoon, Charley had made the decision to lock them away at this early hour as a precaution against an early attack. He didn't trust Noah Murphy to keep his word about waiting until nightfall. In a way he hoped the outlaw would attack early just to relieve the awful tension of waiting.

Rand Cantrell had assembled his men in the Lodgepole; already some of them were on the roof of the building, keeping watch over the road leading from the mountains to the town. Charley was glad they were being so attentive and taking the attack seriously, but the more he looked at the group, the more a nagging worry ate at his mind.

All of the men Rand Cantrell was controlling were those with the history of being town troublemakers; each of them had at one time or another spent a night in jail, courtesy of Charley Hanna. And some had even voiced threats against the marshal. That had never greatly bothered Charley before, for drunks and scoundrels were always quicker with words than they were with action, but in the situation of battle he wasn't sure how cooperative those men would be with the rest of the fighters. And there was always the remote possibility that one of them might use the confusion of battle as a cover for a quick shot at the marshal himself.

That was a thought that had passed only quickly

through Charley's mind but, passing though it was, it bothered him. But there was nothing he could do to protect himself against that possibility, so he forced himself to not worry about it.

It was almost two o'clock before he found time for his midday meal. He headed over to the jailhouse to fry up a few strips of bacon, trying to recall as he walked across the street whether or not he had eaten that last can of beans.

He opened the jailhouse door and was startled to see Sarah leaning over the stove, stirring a pot of stew.

"Sarah! When did you come in here?"

The slender young lady turned and smiled at the marshal. "A little while ago. I knew you would be needing some lunch, and that you would be too busy to fix anything worthwhile yourself. Sit down. This stew is almost ready."

Charley grinned, tossing his hat to the peg on the wall. "You know, I should thrash you for bein' here. I told you to get into the boarding house with the others."

"Hush. You aren't going to thrash anybody. Now sit down like I told you and get ready to eat this while it's hot."

Charley's brows lifted for a moment. No point in arguing with Sarah—she was determined for him to enjoy a good meal, it seemed. And he wasn't going to dissappoint her.

"Here you go, Charley," she said, carrying a bowl of the hot stew to the desk where Charley had sat down. "Hot and ready to eat. I'll get you some coffee in just a second, and here's some biscuits—cold, I'm afraid."

Charley smiled at the slender young woman. "Lord a'mighty—I didn't expect such a feast! Sit down and join me, would you?"

She shrugged. "Why not? I could use a good

meal. . .and I'm used to my own cooking."

The pair set in to the stew as if they hadn't eaten in a week. Sarah had done a good job—seasoning the stew just like Charley liked it—and before they realized it the pair of them had eaten the entire potful. Charley took his last scrap of biscuit and sopped up the remaining traces of stew on his tin plate.

"Awful good, Sarah. Awful good."

"I'm glad you thought so. It's been a long time since I've cooked for a man."

It seemed that as Sarah made her last statement a trace of sadness momentarily entered her mind. Her eye clouded, and for a brief instant her thoughts were transported back to her departed husband.

Charley sensed her mind drifting off, and there was a jolt of something like jealousy in his heart, followed immediately by guilt. He frowned. The feelings running through him were confusing, even though brief in duration. Sarah looked up at him; her eyes cleared, and she was back in the world of the present. Charley felt a strange and profound relief.

"I'm glad you liked the meal," Sarah repeated.

"It was great, the best I've had in months, I guess. And it was a good break from all this tension."

Sarah nodded philosophically. "I know what you mean. It kind of gets to a person after awhile, doesn't it? I mean, in the last couple of days I've felt like. . .oh, but listen to me. It isn't me that's had problems, it's you. I've got no right to complain. I'm sorry."

"No, no, don't be. It's been hard on all of us. And until this night is over things are just goin' to get more that way. It's just now sinkin' in to some of the folks here that this town is goin' to be attacked. It's not just a bad dream—it's real. God knows I wish it wasn't."

Sarah smiled weakly. When she spoke her voice was low, almost cracking.

"Charley, I hope you know I appreciate all you've done for me over these last few days. I don't know what I would have done if you hadn't been around helping me out."

Charley appeared almost embarrassed by her words. Almost like a clumsy, bashful schoolboy, in spite of his broad and muscled shoulders and scraggly beard. "Heck, Sarah, I ain't done nothin' but my job."

Faint and thin was her voice. "Is that all?"

Charley found in himself the courage to look into her eyes. He found the limpid green orbs to be like probes looking into his soul, searching desperately for answers he wasn't sure he had. He felt vaguely uncomfortable.

"No, Sarah. I reckon I was doin' more than my job. I've known that all along."

He stood, unwilling to endure the intensity of her gaze. "These last few days have drawn me close to you. . .close in a way different than anything I've ever felt for a woman. In all my days I've never been able to look a woman in the eye without turning red or babbling like a fool. Lord knows I'm no good at romantic talk. I reckon what I'm trying to say is that I think I'm fallin' in love with you. There—that's it. I never figured I could say nothin' like that to a woman."

Sarah stared at Charley, who still stood with his back toward her. Rising, she moved toward him.

"Charley, do you think I haven't known? The times you've put your arm around me these last days, the way you protected me from those men. I've known how you felt. You don't have to be shy about it."

Charley turned and looked into her face. Her eyes were wide, shining, looking like nothing he had ever seen, shimmering like the stars above the mountains on an icy winter night when the sky is clear and pure. He found himself entranced, almost as if hypnotized by their light.

"And how do you feel, Sarah? Is there any chance at all that you might love me?"

Sarah smiled at him in a way that made his skin tingle. "Charley, is there any way I couldn't?"

"You mean. . ."

"Do you want me to come out and say it? Do you want me to come right out and tell you I love you?"

"I don't know, Sarah, maybe I do."

"All right, then, Charley Hanna, I love you. I truly do love you."

Charley felt weak and incredibly happy. He felt as if his soul could float right out of his body, so enraptured was he. "And I love you, too, Sarah. I figured I probably would bust before I could get up the nerve to tell you. Lord have mercy, I love you more than I can say!"

"Then don't say—just show me."

Charley drew the lovely, green-eyed lady to him, and his lips pressed to hers. For a long time they kissed, Charley feeling a kind of warmth he had never felt before, and Sarah so captivated by his touch and the feeling of his lips against hers that she didn't even notice the bone-crushing grip he had on her or the way his whiskers scratched her delicate skin.

When at last he pulled away his eyes were shining and his breath was coming fast. "I never thought I could feel like I do now."

"Me either. Here, let's sit down before we get so giddy we trip all over the furniture."

The couple moved over to the short bench against the wall and sat down. Charley put his arm over Sarah and pulled her close. For a time they said nothing, then at last Charley spoke.

"Sarah, if I survive this thing—this fight tonight—I'd sure be honored if you would give thought to. . .to marryin' me."

Sarah turned and looked into his eyes. "I'll be glad to marry you, Charley. When it's over—just as soon as it's over. And don't you even talk like you might not survive. Don't you even think it."

"A man has to face the possibilities, Sarah, wait a minute. Did you say. . ."

"I sure did."

Charley's burly arms wrapped around Sarah's delicate frame, squeezing her so hard she couldn't even get the breath to tell him he was on the verge of cracking her ribs. But so happy was she—so intensely, overwhelmingly happy—that she hardly cared.

Chapter 13

Night fell on Dry Creek, and still the town waited. No movement in the hills, no hint of coming danger. The street was lit with torches; men roamed about the street, rifles in their hands. Most were smoking; all were nervous. The wind had stilled, though the air was biting cold. But in spite of the low temperature many of the waiting defenders of the town continually wiped beads of sweat from their brows.

Charley was among those on the street, and he paced back and forth without any clear aim. All that could be done in preparation for the attack had been done. Riflemen watched the torch-lit scene below them from the windows of the boarding house and the Mansfield Saloon; Rand Cantrell's men did the same from the roof of the Lodgepole. Some were inside the log building, Cantrell himself gripping a Winchester at a small window near the corner of the building.

The younger men of the town had been given the task of guarding the alleyways through which the Murphy gang might find entrance should they make it past the other defenders to the rear of the rows of buildings. The narrow alleys were packed with anything that might stop a bullet, and the young men crouched behind the barricades with pale faces and trembling fingers wrapped around the stocks of their rifles. Many times the youths had talked of the countless tales of battle and

126

life-and-death conflicts that had made up the history of the West. But now the excitement was gone, replaced only by overwhelming dread and the fear that they might not be alive to see the morning.

Doc Hopkins was in the boarding house with the rest of the townspeople present, but he knew that once the battle began he would have plenty to do. He kept his black bag close beside his feet, and in a clean cloth sack beside him were heaps of fresh bandages, ready for use.

Preacher Bartlett was moving about, giving words of encouragement to distraught women who had husbands and sons out on the street or in one of the buildings, preparing to defend the town. But there was little he could do but express hope or breathe a short prayer with those who desired it.

Old men with pale eyes and hollow faces stirred restlessly, looking back on days when they had been young, knowing that a few years before they would have been among the men out on the street. And for many of them, it was a time of conflicting feelings. They coveted the safety of this back room, yet also they felt the natural urge to join the younger men of the town in defending those they loved.

Sarah fidgeted in her seat in the boarding house, longing to be near Charley. The knowledge that he loved her, and that he desired to marry her, was a source of intense joy to her, yet she could not shove his words from her mind: "if I survive." She squeezed her eyes shut and prayed with all her heart that Charley would be spared death in the coming battle.

An hour passed after the darkness had settled in, yet still there was no sign of an attack. Out on the street Bo Myers moved over to Charley's side. "Do you think that maybe they gave up the idea?"

The marshal shook his head slowly. "There's hardly a thing in this world I wouldn't give if I thought that could be true," he said. "But I just can't believe they would back out on the fight. Not after all they've done."

"I reckon you're right. I had just hoped that maybe. . ."

"I know the feelin', Bo. Who knows? Maybe they have backed out. But I wouldn't bet on it."

Martin Arlo stepped from the door of the Mansfield Saloon and walked over to where the pair stood. "Everything is ready in there, or at least as ready as it ever will be. In fact, everybody's gettin' a little restless."

"Tell 'em to be patient. They'll have their action soon enough, I'll wager."

"What's Rand been up to? Given any trouble?"

Charley glanced toward the Lodgepole. "Ain't heard a peep out of him since dark. I reckon he's ready to fight along with all of us. I just hope he has the sense to give the right orders. Once this fight starts I don't figure them boys of his will be listening to me."

The three turned and stared down the street, the eerie flicker of the torches illuminating the stretch of snow-covered dirt to the edge of town, where the feeble light faded into darkness. It was an ominous darkness, one that could hide a large band of men. Charley wondered if perhaps Noah Murphy was nearer than he had thought.

As if in answer there came arcing from the darkness a glowing something that fizzled and sputtered. Almost to the barricade it flew, and when it struck the ground and rolled to a stop Charley found himself staring numbly at a bottle well-stuffed with gunpowder, the fuse fizzling down to the last inch. For an instant his muscles seemed frozen and rigid, then at the last possible second he broke through his strange paralysis and flung himself directly into Martin Arlo, grabbing Bo with his free hand. The trio fell to the earth as a tremendous blast lit up the street, kicking dirt and broken glass everywhere, shivering but not breaking the barricade.

Martin Arlo had fallen onto his back, and he stared upward to see a rain of dirt and grit pouring down toward him. "Lord a'mighty. . ." His mouth was choked with dirt and gravel, muffling any other words.

From the darkness at the end of the street bursts of light erupted, the roar of the gunfire echoing from the sides of the buildings. The siege of Dry Creek had begun.

Charley leaped to his feet, bending over from the waist to keep his head below the top of the barricade. Bo Myers picked himself up, dusting off his clothing and looked stunned. Men rushed to the barricade, thrusting rifle muzzles over the heaped up furniture, feed sacks, and overturned wagons.

The roaring of the rifles filled the streets, blocking out the shouts and screams of the men crouching behind the barricades and the townspeople hidden in the back room of the boarding house. Bullets smacked into the barricade, and dirt kicked up in the street from shots that struck short.

Charley raised himself up over the edge of the wagon which sat on its side before him, dirt and rock heaped up against its vertically inclined bed to stop the bullets that ripped through the wood. He caught sight of the flash of fire from the edge of the old, deserted livery on that end of the street, and he sent a bullet winging toward the spot.

He ducked down and looked around him. All along the length of the barricade men were crouched, pouring a stream of lead toward the dark end of the street where the Murphys were hidden. From the windows of the Ketchum Boarding House rifle muzzles protruded, belching forth streams of fire and smoke, the noise of the flying lead singing into the night.

From atop the Lodgepole other rifles flared. Charley saw Joe Marcus toward the west end of the flat roof, squinting down the muzzle of his rifle. There was a sudden burst of fire from the end of the street, and Marcus's hat flipped from his head, falling all the way to the street. The young man ducked to his belly on the roof, suddenly conscious of how close he had come to taking a bullet in the head.

Charley leaned back up against the wagon, sending two more shots down toward the deserted livery. In the lightning flashes of fire that erupted on the dark street he made out the quickly moving forms of men. Just how many he could not tell. Noah Murphy was said to lead a large group, and from the amount of gunfire pouring in from the darkness Charley suspected that the rumors were true.

The bottle bomb had confirmed his fear that the Murphys had the powder from Novak's gunsmithy. So far that one bomb had been all that had been set off, but Novak had said that there were several kegs of powder buried behind the shop. With all that powder at their disposal, the Murphy gang could cause more trouble than the town was prepared to handle.

Bo Myers scrambled to Charley's side. "What are we goin' to do about them bombs, Charley? If they hit this barricade. . ."

"There ain't much we can do, Bo. Whoa! Here comes another one!"

The whiskey bottle arched through the darkness, landing about twenty feet from the barricade. Almost before he thought, Charley stood upright, dangerously exposing his head and arms above the line of the barricade, and then he squeezed down on the trigger of his rifle.

The shot hit the bottle squarely, shattering it and

sending powder in all directions. When the flaring fuse lit it there was no explosion, only the burning of the powder, illuminating the street all around. Charley ducked back down, grinning.

"There's one that won't blow," he said. "Let's try to do that every chance we get."

"It ain't always gonna be easy, Charley."

A loud cry cut off Charley's reply. The marshal jerked his head around to find from where it had come, and his eyes caught sight of one of Cantrell's men pitching forward from the Lodgepole roof to sprawl out in the snow on the opposite side of the barricade. Charley thought at first that the man was Dry Creek's first fatality, but then he moaned and moved slightly.

"He's alive!" said Charley. "Bo, go get the Doc, real quick!"

The deputy scurried off toward the boaring house, keeping his head low. Charley braced himself to leap over the wagon and race toward the wounded man, but Martin Arlo's hand gripped his shoulder.

"No, Charley—let me do it."

And before Charley could answer, Martin Arlo had vaulted over the barricade and was racing toward the fallen man. Charley stood transfixed for a moment, stunned by the sudden action, then he saw the increased burst of fire from the end of the street, and the dirt around Arlo's heels began kicking up.

"Keep him covered!" shouted Charley. "Pour it on!"

In obedience to his own order, the marshal stood upright and sent a steady stream of hot lead toward the dark end of the street. All along the barricade others did the same, and from the roof of the Lodgepole and the second-story windows on the facing street also added their blitz of lead to the battle.

The flashing, roaring explosions of Murphy gunfire

were snuffed suddenly, the outlaws obviously ducking under cover, shocked by the sudden outpour of bullets. Arlo made it over to the side of the fallen man, kneeling and looking at an ugly, bleeding chest wound that had punctured the lung.

"Move your butt back here, Arlo!" shouted Charley. "Don't sit there lookin' him over!"

Arlo reached down and slipped his hand under the man's knees, placing the other under his shoulders. As gently as he could he picked him up, scurrying more slowly this time toward the middle of the barricade. Charley stood and took the wounded man from Arlo, moving gingerly yet carefully toward the boarding house. Arlo scrambled to safety just as Doc Hopkins moved to the door of the boarding house, Bo just behind him. The blitz of fire ceased as suddenly as it had begun, and for a moment the town was engulfed in an almost eerie silence.

"Move him in here," Doc ordered during that silence. "Lay him on the couch."

Outside there was a horrific, tremendous blasting noise, and the building shook suddenly. Charley almost lost his balance with the wounded man in his arms, and the sound of frightened yells came from the back room of the boarding house.

"What is it now?" he muttered, laying the man down on the couch. He dashed toward the door, followed by Bo Myers.

A portion of the barricade had been blown away, obviously by one of the bottle bombs. Several of the men who had been fighting from behind the barricade were desperately trying to patch it together again, gathering up feed sacks with half of their contents blown out, piecing together the wall of furniture that now was blown partly into splinters. And the Murphys were taking advantage of the confusion, pouring a harder rain of fire down upon Dry Creek's besieged defenders.

Charley ran toward the gap in the barricade, preparing to help rebuild it as best he could. But another bottle came arcing through the night, to fall with torchlight gleaming upon its side almost in the midst of the men.

"Clear out! Out!" he cried, leaping toward the bottle.

His fingers closed around it, and he cast it back over the barricade just as the fuse burned down to the powder. The blast sent glass and pebbles flying in all directions, the concussion shattering the glass in the windows of the jailhouse office.

"Boys, in case you didn't know it, that was a close one," Charley said. "Way too close."

The men moved to pick up the portions of the barricade that had been in their hands when the second bottle had fallen. As best they could they rebuilt the barricade, keeping their heads low to avoid the bullets that whizzed above them. Meanwhile the men in the second-story windows and atop the Lodgepole kept on shooting toward the deserted livery where the Murphys were making their battle station.

Another bottle came flying over the barricade, landing not five feet behind Charley. The marshal dropped his rifle and dodged toward the bottle, but before he could reach it something leaped in front of him, knocking him aside.

It was Bo Myers. The young deputy grabbed the bottle, but he did not throw it back over the barricade as Charley had done. Instead he grasped the fuse and yanked it out of the bottle, stomping it out beneath his boot.

Charley smiled. "Good thinkin', Bo. Now maybe we can turn some of their tactics against them."

Bo picked up the burned out fuse and slipped it back

133

into the bottle, using a piece of the splintered barricade to pack the powder and rock down tight again. "Let's just hold this until we got a better shot at them Murphys," he said, slipping the bottle, a flat, flash-style whiskey bottle, into his coat pocket.

In the darkness of the deserted livery, Noah Murphy was frowning. Around him his men were firing into the barricade, sending occasional shots toward the figures that bobbed up on the roof of the Lodgepole Saloon or out of the windows in the other buildings across the street. But so far their shots had done little good, dropping only one man. Even the hand bombs had not had the effect Noah Murphy had thought they would.

"Stop your shootin'!" the outlaw leader cried. His men went on shooting, either not having heard or not heeding his command.

"Stop! I said stop shootin'!" he cried. This time his men obeyed, looking at him inquiringly.

"But Noah, I though we was supposed to—"

"Shut up. It's obvious we ain't doin' much good like this. We'll just shoot out our ammunition and waste our bombs and that'll be the end of it. It's time to use the keg."

One of the outlaws, a fat, bearded man with a slight limp, grinned at the mention of the keg. He had been waiting for this moment ever since Noah Murphy had first come up with the idea. And so he moved quickly to where the barrel sat in the corner of the old stable.

It was one of the kegs of powder, about half the powder removed and the empty space filled with rocks and bits of broken glass. A long fuse extended through a hole in the lid of the barrel.

Noah Murphy quickly inspected the barrel. The powder was packed tightly, the rocks and glass around the outside. They would make devastating missiles when the powder blew. If the barrel could be rolled just right, in just the right direction, then the barricade would be blown to the sky, perhaps along with several of the buildings around it. Then the people of Dry Creek would learn what a real siege was all about.

"Mickey, I'm gonna give you the privilege of bein' the one to roll this here barrel out there," Murphy said. "And you'd best do it right, 'cause the rest of the powder is in the hand bombs. This is our one shot to get through that barricade."

The fat outlaw grinned. For his simple mind, rolling the barrel was like a game, and being allowed to do the honors was a privilege he craved. "All right, Noah. I'll do it. I'll do it good."

The other outlaws glanced at each other, smiling. Heading out into that street would be like walking into a deathtrap. No one else craved that duty. If this ignorant, half-witted Mickey wanted the job, he could have it.

Noah hustled the fat man over to the door of the livery. He glanced down the street. The sudden ceasing of fire had obviously confused the men defending the main street, for he could see heads peering cautiously over the barricade and out of the windows of the buildings. He didn't expect Mickey to survive. But that didn't bother him, so long as the fat man managed to successfully get the powder barrel rolling.

"Mickey—roll that barrel as hard and fast as you can right toward that corner of the barricade. When it blows it should rip out that barricade and blow the front off that saloon and maybe off the boardin' house too. But you gotta roll it just right, and roll it hard."

"I can do it, Noah. I'll do it just like you want me to."

Noah grinned and slapped the fat man on the back. "I'm sure you will, Mickey. I'm sure you will."

The outlaw reached into his pocket and struck it on

his heel. He stuck the tip to the fuse until it began flaring. Then he kicked open the rotting old livery door and pointed down the street.

"Roll, Mickey! Let it roll!"

Chapter 14

Charley Hanna saw the barrel rolling toward the barricade and comprehended its significance just as a dozen rifles blasted, knocking the outlaw rolling the barrel to his back in the snow, where he lay and moved no more.

When he fell his boot struck the barrel, knocking it off its course and sending it to where the corner of the barricade bucked up against the porch of the jailhouse. Charley heard himself shouting a loud cry of warning to the men on that side of the barricade and in the windows of the saloon adjacent to the jail, at the same time throwing himself to the dirt and wrapping his arms around his head, knowing that he could never make it to the other side of the street in time to escape the concussion of the impending blast. For a brief moment just before the flaring fuse burnt down to the powder there was a period of almost total silence in the town—a strangely peaceful silence.

And a silence that was short-lived. The blast that rendered the barrel was spectacular, immense, deafening beyond anything Charley had ever imagined. He was conscious of the stinging feeling of scattering dirt particles burying themselves in the skin of his arms as if fired from some giant scattergun; the horrible jolting shock of the force of the explosion as it ripped across the street; the sudden rendering of the barricade into a roaring, dark storm of splinters, dirt, and flying brick; the sight of a body being flipped through the air like a ragdoll in a tornado.

Charley was conscious in the confusion of the porch of the jailhouse collapsing and the right corner of the Mansfield Saloon being shredded into a huge, gaping hole. He heard men atop the Lodgepole Saloon crying out as bits of flying wood struck them, and a body pitched forward off the roof to flop into the snow. The barricade was half destroyed, the entire right end of it blown into pieces. From the interior of the boarding house came the shouts of men who had been terror-struck by the blast, and mingled with their voices came the more muffled cries of the women shivering in the back rooms of the boarding house.

Charley was stunned, his head reeling where he had struck it against the corner of a barrel as he fell. Everywhere there was grit, choking and stinging, and Charley found himself so addled he couldn't even force himself to rise.

Something struck the ground beside him—a bottle, filled with powder, the fuse fizzling horrifyingly close to the dark grains. For a moment he stared blankly at it, hardly able to focus his eyes, then he forced his hand outward and it closed numbly around the bottle. He threw it blindly over the barricade just as the fuse burned all the way down.

The bottle exploded before it struck the ground, the flash lighting up the street and the roar echoing down the row of buildings. But after the magnificent blast of moments before, it seemed hardly more than the popping of a child's firecracker.

Almost simultaneously there came another rending blast, this one on the other side of the barricade. Bits of shattered furniture, ruptured feed sacks, and a wagon wheel flew into the air. Three men, staggered by the previous blast and leaning up against the barricade, were knocked backwards by the force of the explosion. Charley groaned and forced his torso upward so he could look at the results of the blast. The barricade was almost totally gone now, a weak, scattered remnant of what it had been before, and the men that had been knocked back by the final blast were lying too still for comfort.

There was the sudden noise of horses racing toward the barricade from the darkness, and the clatter of blasting rifles filled the air. Charley pushed himself upward to glance over the barricade portion that was left in front of him, then he ducked down as quickly again.

The horse and rider leaped over him, the rear hooves of the animal scarcely missing his legs. Two other riders galloped down the middle of the street in the confusion and sea of smoke, and Charley could see the flaring bombs in their hands. His hand groped for his pistol just as one of the riders heaved the bomb he was holding through a window in the Ketchum Boarding House, while the others tossed their bottles through the windows of the Mansfield Saloon.

Charley fired his pistol almost blindly as the front of the saloon buckled outward from the force of the blast, and when he opened his eyes he saw the riderless horse loping in fright farther down the street. But the two other riders had wheeled their mounts around and were headed straight back toward the stunned defenders of the shattered barricade, this time with their pistols drawn.

Charley rolled to one side to escape being pounded by the hooves of the horse that ran straight at him, and he fired a quick and useless shot at the rider, who returned the fire toward him. But the shot missed, and the rider moved on past Charley, riding through a gap in the barricade.

Charley forced himself to his feet, then moved at a crouch toward the three men that lay still where they had fallen after the bottle had exploded in their faces. He ducked when he heard the singing of lead overhead, for the Murphy gang was doing its best to pick off the men in the street. Already most had darted over to the boarding house, which still retained its front wall only because the bomb which had been tossed through window had somehow not worked properly, the fuse burning out without setting off the powder.

Charley knelt beside the man, and Martin Arlo, pale-faced and trembling, crouched beside him.

"He's in a bad way, Martin. You carry him in. I'll check the others."

Arlo put his hands under the man's arms, lifting him as gently as possible by the armpits and dragging him toward the Ketchum Boarding House. To take him to the saloon would be almost useless, for though the building was closer, the front wall was gone, spread across the street, and most of the men who had been firing from the front window had either been stunned or knocked completely out. Martin Arlo suspected as he dragged the wounded man toward the boarding house that a few of them might even have been killed.

Charley came darting up beside Arlo just as the man dragged a wounded comrade inside the boarding house door. A bullet smacked into the doorjamb beside Charley's head, and he ducked as he moved into the building.

"There ain't nothin' to do for the others," he said. "They didn't survive it."

Doc Hopkins moved over from the couch against the opposite wall, where the other wounded man lay, his

140

chest tightly bandaged and his face the image of death. But he was breathing faintly, and for now that would have to do. Doc had others to tend to.

"Where do you want him, Doc?"

"Over yonder on that blanket. There on the floor."

Martin Arlo moved the man over while Charley replaced the spent cartridge in his pistol. He was worrying about the men next door in the Mansfield Saloon, for the double blast which had ripped through the building had been of devastating force. Charley feared the worst. There were hardly any shots being fired from the building, and even the men on the second floor were in no good position to fight, for the blast had kicked out most of the supports of the floor, and the ceiling threatened to cave in on the wounded and stunned men on the lower level. And the sagging floor was so weakened toward the front of the building that the men on the second level could not draw close enough to the windows to fire for fear their weight would break the floor beneath them.

Charley dropped his pistol into his holster and moved back toward the front door, preparing to dart around and enter the Mansfield Saloon. He moved over to the open door, peered cautiously around it, then moved.

Sarah Redding watched him exit from her position at the door of the rear kitchen of the boarding house, and her lip trembled. She glanced at Doc, whose shirt and vest were now bespeckled with blood, and she felt suddenly faint.

Charley moved along the boardwalk, almost tripping over a shattered piece of the saloon wall that had buckled out across his path. He saw from the corner of his eye the flashing of rifle fire from the empty livery where the Murphy gang was holed up, and lead smacked into the porch column beside him.

He darted into the shell of the Mansfield Saloon,

shocked by what he saw.

The place was a heap of rubble. The remaining men that were capable of fighting had moved toward the front of the building and were crouching behind whatever cover was available and firing in the direction of the Murphy gang. Many others were laying about, some wounded, three dead. Charley felt intense anger. So far the Murphys had managed to do more damage in a few minutes than Charley would have anticipated they could do in several hours.

"Bo!"

"I'm here, Charley."

The deputy came around the corner from the alley between the damaged jailhouse and the saloon, leaping into the frontless building before the Murphys had time to take aim at him. In the confusion of the last minutes Charley had lost track of his deputy.

"Charley, that powder they got is killin' us." Bo glanced at the still body of a man half-covered with rubble. "And that ain't just a way of speakin'."

"You still got that bottle of powder?"

"Yeah. You got an idea?"

Charley frowned. "I don't know. . .maybe."

"What is it you have in mind?"

Charley didn't get a chance to answer the question, for there was a sudden chattering of riflefire from the top of the Lodgepole. Charley headed for the corner of the building, realizing only then that he had dropped his rifle outside and neglected to pick it up in the confusion. Quickly he drew his .44.

The men atop the Lodgepole were firing in the same general direction as before, but this time they were aiming across the street from the empty livery.

"Some of 'em must have crossed the street," Charley said. "Could be that they're gettin' ready to sneak around behind."

Bo glanced carefully around the edge of the building. "Yeah I can see somebody movin' around just around the edge of the jail."

"Then I reckon they are tryin' to move around behind. . .Bo!"

Charley's mouth dropped open as the deputy suddenly moved forward, scooping up something off the boardwalk. A bullet thunked into the boardwalk at his feet, and he moved back in, his fingers pinching at something.

"Got another one, Charley! Got another one!" He proudly held up another powder-filled bottle, the fuse snuffed out by his fingers just above the mouth of the bottle.

"Good job, Bo! Great!"

"That makes two of 'em. Might come in handy."

There was the sound of a single rifle firing, fast and desperately. Charley tensed, drew his pistol, then began moving toward the front of the building, cutting around to the left, at the same time barking an order.

"Smith, Adams—come with me—Jackson, Marvin, you too. I think we got trouble!"

The men moved quickly and followed Charley around the front of the boarding house and toward the alley between it and the next building. They met a frightened young man moving out of the alley. Charley slipped his pistol into his holster long enough to grab the young man's shoulders and stop him.

A pale face stared up into his eyes. "They're comin'. . .comin' through the alley!"

Charley shoved the young man aside and leaped directly in front of the alley. A figure was clambering up onto the barricade which blocked it. Charley's gun whipped out, and a quick shot knocked the figure back. Charley heard a man behind the figure grunt as the body struck him. The marshal leaped to the side, concealing himself behind the corner of the adjoining building, motioning for the others to stay clear of the alley entrance.

There was a sudden burst of fire from the old livery where the Murphys had been hidden. Charley frowned and ducked down to avoid the bullets that slapped the wall above him.

"They split up—and here we are stuck in the open!"

The men broke and ran with sudden panic, although Charley shouted for them to try to retain some sort of order. But in the midst of all the battle confusion, orders were useless. The men scattered to various points all along the other side of the street, making them safe for a time from the gunfire from the livery, but also clearing the way for the members of the Murphy gang who were trying to enter the alley.

Charley dropped to his belly, rolling until he could fire a quick shot into the alleyway at the men who once more were attempting to clamber over the barricade. He rolled back quickly as a bullet struck the dirt at his side, then he rose and ran at a crouch back toward the boarding house. It was no use to remain where he was; the Murphys had free access now through the alley, and to try to stop them alone would be suicide.

He darted into the boarding house door, finding the room filled with wounded men and pale women who were attempting to help Doc Hopkins as he made his rounds around the makeshift hospital. A few of the men who had been fighting earlier behind the barricade now were crouched at the windows, peering out at the Murphy gang, wanting to fire but fearing they might draw return fire which could be devastating to Doc's efforts to help the wounded.

Charley could hear the sound of the Murphy men mounting the barricade in the alley beside the building. Sudden rage raced through him, and he raised the muzzle of his pistol to the wall and fired a blind shot directly through the side of the building.

He heard the grunting sound of a man on the other side and knew his shot had struck home. Then suddenly there was the noise of rifle fire directly overhead, and further shouts from the alley.

Charley froze, then his face broke into a smile. He darted toward the back stairs, racing up them and into the second floor hallway. He glanced down the length of the hall and saw the wooden ladder which led through an angled doorway onto the roof. The door was open.

Charley climbed the ladder and peered out over the edge of the sloping door until he caught sight of Bo Myers kneeling beside the edge of the building, firing his rifle downward. The deputy would fire a shot, pull back as he avoided the return fire, then lever another shell into his rifle chamber and fire once more.

Charley raced to the deputy's side and glanced into the dark alley. The last of the men were moving out of the rear of the alleyway as quickly as they could, their plan to mount the barricade forgotten. The sudden appearance of Bo on the rooftop had provided quite an effective deterrent against any further action, and the crumpled bodies lying across the barricade and in the dirt behind it were ample evidence of the devastation the young deputy had rendered.

The five remaining Murphy gunmen darted back toward an old log shed that backed up the building just across the alley, and when they had forced their way inside a sudden volley of lead winged over Charley's head. The marshal and his deputy dropped to their bellies on the flat roof, unable to rise due to the singing bullets that passed scarcely a foot over their heads. And the noise of increased shooting from the street behind them let them know that the battle at that point had increased in intensity.

Charley caught sight of Bo fumbling in his pocket, and the deputy suddenly produced one of the bottles he had intercepted. Charley dug in his pocket for the matches he always carried, and he shoved the box over to Bo.

The deputy struck the match against the edge of the roof, shielding the flame with the palm of his other hand. He glanced at Charley.

"Wish me luck!" And he lit the short fuse.

There wasn't time to move slowly and carefully, for the fuse was almost burned down to the powder by the time he had flipped the match away. Without regard to the bullets whistling around him, Bo raised up and flipped the bottle toward the shed which held the gunmen.

The bottle struck the wall of the shed just above the single open window of the crude structure, then it fell to balance precariously on the sill before tipping backwards into the little building.

Bo dropped back down to his belly just as the bottle exploded, shattering the little shed into splinters. Bits of wood flew high into the air behind the building, and snow and splinters rained down on the marshal and his deputy. Then there was sudden silence.

Charley raised his head and shook the dirt from his hair. The noise of shooting from the main street behind them had stopped. The stillness of the night was so intense that it almost roared in his ears.

"Bo, there's no more fightin'. Do you think. . ."

They moved across the roof and peered over the raised front of the building to the street. There was no more gunfire erupting from the old livery. The men atop the Lodgepole were sitting in silent vigil, their rifles gripped tightly. But there was no shooting. The street, torchlit and strewn with rubble and occasional bodies, was silent.

Dry Creek had survived the first round of the Murphy siege. Charley sighed and sank down to sit on his haunches, listening to the sound of his loudly beating heart.

Chapter 15

The town fell into a strange combination of elation and despair, and the faces of the men who ventured into the street to gather the bodies of the dead were alternately lit with relieved smiles or twisted with revulsion. The horror of the death all around took its toll on all, and many were the wailed cries of those who had lost husbands, sons, brothers in the fight, but the joy of continued life was almost as overwhelming for the men who only minutes before had not been sure they would live to see the next hour.

But Charley, relieved though he was that the siege was at least temporarily stopped, reminded all those around him that there was no reason to suppose the fight was over. Just why Noah Murphy had chosen to withdraw the marshal wasn't certain; perhaps it was because the attempt to send part of his men into town through the alley had failed, or perhaps the outlaw simply didn't like his fighting position. But Charley suspected that the withdrawal from battle would only lead to an even more deadly attack as soon as Murphy could develop another scheme.

Based on what Novak had said about the amount of powder that had been stolen from his shop, Charley was sure Murphy had more on hand. It was the gunpowder that was destroying the town, for the defenders had nothing of equal power to throw back at the Murphys.

The destruction of the barricade had shown how quickly the Murphys could overthrow what feeble defenses the town could throw up. Charley considered ordering the barricade rebuilt, but he decided against it. What the Murphys had done once they could do again, and it might be better to spend the time refortifying the buildings rather than trying to gather together the shattered remnant of the barricade.

Charley walked into the boarding house to see how Doc was doing with the wounded. He found the front room of the house even more crowded than it had been before, for several of the men who had taken slight wounds had come in to have them patched. Most had been unwilling to leave their posts during the fighting.

"How's it goin,' Doc?"

The old man glanced irritably at the marshal. "How do you think? Leave me alone. I got no time to waste talking."

The old doctor moved away, and Charley smiled faintly. The old codger was irritable enough, but he had good reason. Charley could see that he was doing as well as he could with the wounded, and he determined to leave him to his work.

Sarah Redding approached him. She looked pale and frightened, but also happy to see Charley. He turned to her and opened his arms, and she darted into his embrace. He squeezed her close, patting the back of her head with his rugged hand.

"Is it over, Charley?"

"For a while. But they'll be back."

Sarah's expression reflected despair. "Back. . .but I thought that just maybe they had given up. Oh, Charley, I don't know how much more of this I can take. So many have been killed for no reason. Isn't there something we can do short of starting up the fighting again?"

149

Charley shook his head. "No, Sarah. The time for talk is over. And Noah Murphy has got his heart set on burnin' the town. There's nothin' we can do but fight it out 'til the end."

Sarah's face reddened, and she appeared almost angry. "But it's so absurd! So ridiculous! Why should more die? Is anything in this world worth that?"

"I don't know, Sarah. It ain't a question of what's worth what or why others should die. It's just a matter of what is."

Sarah looked away. "Is it that simple? Folks are going to die and that's all there is to it?"

"I know it sounds cruel."

"I can't believe there's nothing we can do. I just can't believe it." And she turned and stalked away. Charley looked after her, somewhat taken aback. He hadn't expected such an outburst from her. He put it down to tension and forgot about it, moving out into the street.

Rand Cantrell watched the marshal through the small window at which he had remained throughout the battle. He had fired an occasional shot in the midst of the fighting, but for the most part he had tried to stay as safe as he could without looking as if he was doing so. He had been as surprised by the suddenness of the initial attack as anyone else, and though he refused to admit it to himself, he had been extremely frightened throughout the fight. He didn't envy Charley Hanna's position out there on the street. He preferred to do his fighting behind thick walls.

The marshal disappeared into the bomb-ravaged saloon, and Cantrell turned and headed for the back door of the Lodgepole. He went out into the night, the crusty snow crunching beneath his feet, and began climbing the rough ladder which had been set up against the back of the building.

He mounted the top of the roof to be greeted by dark

stares from the men shivering in the wind that whistled down from the mountains and skirted across the flat rooftop. He walked past most of them, heading for where Joe Marcus sat crouched in the corner, his Winchester '73 across his knees. He grunted when he saw the gambler approaching.

"Hello, Joe. Where's your brother?"

The young man gestured over the edge of the roof. Cantrell glanced over and saw a body crumpled against a feedbag that had been a part of the barricade. It was Freddy Marcus.

"What happened?"

"He got shot just after that barrel of powder blew the barricade up," he said. "Shot blew him clean off the roof."

"Sorry."

"Yeah, me too. And I'm gonna make them Murphys sorry, too, if it's the last thing I ever do. Freddy—he never hurt nobody."

"Yeah. I'd say that's right."

Cantrell looked dismayed somehow, and he gazed away from Joe Marcus toward the saloon. The young man caught the distant look in his eye.

"What's wrong? You thinkin' about something?"

The gambler glanced back at the young man, his expression contemplative. After a pause he said, "Yes, Joe. I am." He looked around him. "Can I trust you to not tell anyone about what I'm going to tell you?"

Joe Marcus looked at him intently, his sadness for the loss of his brother being covered over by sudden interest. "Sure, Rand. I can keep a secret."

The gambler placed his hand on the young man's shoulder and pulled him close. He spoke to him in a quiet voice, inches from his ear.

"Your brother and I had a deal, Joe. Something I discussed with him before Murphy showed up. And now

151

that he's—now that he's gone, it sort of messes up my plan."

"What plan?"

Cantrell gazed at the man, as if trying to read something in his face. Apparently satisfied, he again asked if he could trust Joe Marcus to keep a secret.

The young man was becoming intrigued to the point of exasperation. "Sure! Rand, I won't say a word."

"And will you do something for me if I ask you—and pay you well, I might add—to do the same thing Freddy had agreed to do for me?"

The young man looked confused. "What are you talkin' about?"

Cantrell frowned slightly, then began to rise. "Forget it, Joe. It isn't worth it."

"No! Don't leave! I'll do it, whatever it is. Just tell me."

Cantrell studied the man. "Very well, then. I'm giving you the job I had given your brother. I want you to do something for me in the midst of the fighting. . .to make sure of something."

"And what's that?"

"I want you to make certain that Charley Hanna doesn't survive the battle."

An hour passed without any sign of further attack. Charley regrouped the men of the town, with the exception of those who looked to Rand Cantrell for their leadership, and new plans for defense were drawn up. With the barricade destroyed there would be no way to keep the Murphy gang out of the main street. The defenders would have to count on careful shooting to keep the town from being overrun.

But Charley worried silently that with the Murphys still in possession of the gunpowder there would be little they could do. One well-placed bomb in the already damaged saloon could wipe out the building, and if by chance one of the handbombs went off in the boarding house, the blast might kill many of the townsfolk hiding there, as well as the wounded whom Doc was tending. Only by the most daring, accurate shooting possible could the town defenders hope to hold off the attack.

Sarah had returned to the back room of the boarding house after her meeting with Charley, and now she paced nervously about, her movements watched disinterestedly by most of those who kept their nervous vigil there, but watched with much more intensity by Kathy Denning. Kathy had been watching Sarah much of the time over the last hours, and her rage had grown all the while. She pondered over how Sarah had taken the man she secretly loved away from her, and the thought of it nagged at her until she could hardly stand the sight of the slender, lovely lady. But still she felt compelled to stare at her, her feelings smoldering in her like a fire about to explode into full flame.

And at the same time Kathy fought back the feelings of guilt which gnawed at her because of the lies she had spread about Charley Hanna. Ever since her last talk with Rand Cantrell she had been deermined to keep things as they were, but still she was conscious that what she had done was wrong.

Not conscious enough to straighten the facts out, though. If Charley was going to shove her aside like so much trash, then let him suffer in any way she could arrange it!

She wouldn't let herself think about how it hurt her to spread lies about Charley. She wouldn't let herself realize that it did hurt her, for that would rob her of the only outlet she had for her anger.

Kathy Denning had never before been a jealous individual, not until she had seen Charley slipping away from her. In her heart she knew he had never been hers in the first place, but before there had always been the hope that perhaps one day he would be. Now the hope was gone, leaving only an emptiness inside her.

Sarah Redding was standing near the doorway of the room, her arms folded in front of her. And as Kathy stared at her, she suddenly stepped through the doorway and out toward the front of the building, walking with a determined stride.

Kathy frowned. What was she up to? According to Charley Hanna's orders, all the townsfolk who weren't fighting, helping with the wounded, or loading weapons for the fighters were supposed to remain where they were. Kathy hesitated, then curiosity overwhelmed her, and she slipped out of the room after Sarah.

She saw Sarah weaving her way through the makeshift hospital in the main room of the boarding house, then she slipped out the front door. In the bustle and confusion no one seemed to notice, and when Kathy followed after her no one stopped her either.

Kathy looked slyly down the boardwalk. Sarah was slipping toward the saloon, no more than a few yards ahead of her. Kathy ducked back into the shadows and watched Sarah look cautiously around the edge of the almost demolished building, peering into the room as if she were trying to avoid detection.

Strange, Kathy thought. She figured that Sarah had left the room in search of Charley Hanna, but it appeared that she was trying to avoid being spotted by him—or anyone else, for that matter. But why?

Sarah moved quickly across the open front of the saloon, apparently making it without being seen by anyone on the inside, for there was no indication that anyone was trying to stop her, as surely they would have if she had been spotted. Kathy followed to the same point Sarah had been before, then she herself peeped around the corner to peer into the saloon. The torchlight flickered on her auburn hair and cast strange, dancing shadows on the smoke-blackened wall beside her.

The saloon was crowded with fighters, and Kathy could hear the clatter of rifles being loaded and pistols being checked. Faces turned almost toward her, and she ducked back. Glancing down the street, she saw Sarah Redding mounting the boardwalk in front of the jail, moving past the shattered remnant of the barricade.

Now Kathy *was* confused. Sarah Redding was heading out of town, seemingly not even thinking of the Murphy gang, to walk right into their grasp!

A thought entered Kathy's mind, gripping her. She pushed it aside, unwilling to accept it.

She glanced once more into the interior of the saloon. Still the men mingled about, many of them filling ammunition pouches or belts with slugs from several boxes being overseen by gunsmith Novak. She wasn't sure whether or not she could make it across the large gap where the front wall had been without being seen, but she would have to try. Otherwise Sarah would be out of her sight and she would never know the answer to the mystery that was tantalizing her.

She waited a few seconds longer, until it looked as if no one was looking her way, then she darted across the gap. She tried to move swiftly, without actually running, for a blur of motion might catch the attention of someone on the inside. And with nerves on edge as they were, she might even be shot before she was recognized.

Amazingly enough, she made it. She entered an area of thick shadow at the corner of the jail house, and stood panting for a minute, unable to believe she had not been spotted.

The men atop the Lodgepole! She had forgotten them! They had a clear view of the street.

She glanced in that direction, and then sighed. No heads were visible against the blackness of the sky. The men must have moved momentarily off their perch, or at least to the back section of the roof, probably to get fresh ammunition, as the men in the Mansfield Saloon were doing.

Kathy didn't have time to wonder at her own desire for stealth. Somehow she didn't want to be seen; she was overwhelmed with a sense of mystery, and she had a chilling suspicion of just what Sarah Redding was doing. And it filled Kathy with wonderment, and a sense of shame, in spite of the hate she felt for Sarah.

She looked out into the darkness beyond the reach of the flickering torches that lined the street. Sarah had gone into that sea of shadows, and for the moment was lost from sight. She squinted, trying to probe into the murkiness and make out where Sarah had gone.

She caught sight of a fleeting figure, a skirt tossing faintly in the night. Kathy started to move forward in pursuit, then suddenly she pulled herself to a stop.

Another figure was moving on the opposite side of the street, coming around from the rear of the Lodgepole. It was Rand Cantrell, and from the look of things he was heading into the darkness after Sarah.

Kathy felt suddenly chilled. In spite of the fact that Cantrell had provided her, in his willingness to do anything to hurt Charley Hanna, with a welcome tool of revenge against the man who had jilted her, Kathy sensed in the more rational portion of her moral consciousness that the man was evil. He could be planning nothing but wrong toward Sarah Redding.

Peculiar, how that thought made Kathy feel suddenly protective toward the very lady she hated most. . . .

She waited until Cantrell had moved on down the dark street after Sarah, then she followed. She shuddered as she stepped across the bullet-ridden body of the hefty outlaw who had rolled the barrel of gun-powder against the barricade, then she slipped as quietly as possible into a path almost directly behind Rand Cantrell, who clearly had no idea he was being followed.

Sarah had reached the stable where the Murphys had been holed up. Bravely she approached the gaping doorway of the building, and Kathy held her breath in anticipation of a burst of gunfire pouring out of the structure. But it never came. The livery was, to all appearances, deserted.

Kathy paused, tense and breathless, and watched Sarah disappear inside. Rand Cantrell paused at the edge of the door, apparently worried about the possible presence of the outlaw band, but then he entered after Sarah.

Kathy felt her skin crawling. Something drew her toward the stable, regardless of the fact that she felt a strong urge to run back to the safer confines of the guarded street. But instead she stepped silently after Cantrell, vanishing into the shadows inside the empty livery.

Sarah stood in the midst of the livery, looking around her, fear and something like confusion showing in her face. She stared into the darkness of the vacant stalls and peered upward to the black loft.

"Noah Murphy?"

Sarah's voice was thin and trembling, somehow almost childlike. Kathy felt a shiver run through her as she realized what the young widow was doing. It was suddenly hard to hate her.

"Noah Murphy, are you here?" Sarah was trembling from more than the cold.

There was a movement in the shadows. Sarah wheeled around. "Noah Murphy—is that you?"

A figure stepped from the darkness. "Not quite, Mrs.

Redding. Not quite."

Sarah recoiled at the sight of Rand Cantrell's lean figure standing before her. "You. . .what are you doing here? Why did you follow me?"

"Who wouldn't follow a young woman who headed straight for the pit of the viper, so to speak? What are *you* doing here?"

Sarah drew herself up straight. "Do you really want me to tell you that?"

"I asked, didn't I?"

"I came to do what you've been wanting. I came to turn myself over to Noah Murphy."

Chapter 16

Rand Cantrell laughed. "Noble of you, my lady! Such a spirit of self sacrifice!"

Sarah bristled. "How can you make fun of me when you were the one who begged for Charley to turn himself over? What kind of man are you?"

The gambler ignored her. But his hand slipped closer to the .44 in his belt. "I'm afraid I can't let you do that. I have other uses for you."

"What are you talking about?" The young woman inched away from the man, who suddenly seemed to stand several inches taller, every foot of him threatening and cold.

"I'll be needing you later for my own purposes. Sort of a ticket out of town, if it comes to that." His hand grasped the butt of his pistol. "Come with me."

Sarah backed away. "No! I don't know what you want with me, but I have to do what I came for. I won't let you stop me!"

The pistol came out of the holster and leveled at Sarah's abdomen. "I'm afraid you have no choice, Mrs. Redding. You're coming with me."

He lunged forward and his hand gripped roughly on her shoulder. It wasn't a calloused, rough hand like Charley's—the skin was that of a man who knew little real labor, a hand that spent more time delicately caressing a deck of cards than it did gripping a spade or swinging a pick—but it gripped firmly on the small, feminine shoulder of Sarah Redding. With a cry the young widow was pulled roughly into Cantrell's grasp.

"*Let her go!*"

Kathy stepped from the shadows, startling the gambler and making him lose his grip on Sarah. The fleet young woman twisted away from him and half-fell against the wall of an empty stall, panting and afraid.

"You miserable. . .where did you come from!"

"I followed you, you devil. And this time I'm not playing your game. Don't you know we've done enough wrong already? I was a fool to listen to you, and I won't let you do this."

Cantrell's lips spread thin and pale over two rows of even teeth, and his arm whipped back. The hand holding the pistol descended, and the heavy metal of the .44 crashed against Kathy Denning's skull. The auburn-haired woman let out a muffled cry and collapsed senseless to the floor. Sarah tried to scream, but her voice failed her.

"Now you'll come with me," Cantrell grunted, moving forward, not taking even a second glance at Kathy's form crumpled on the floor. He lunged forward and grasped Sarah's arm, pulling her to him. His pistol pressed to her throat.

"Move—and if you make a sound you'll regret it."

Sarah complied, trembling, stumbling along as Cantrell roughly grasped her arm in an intensely painful position. He stopped in the doorway looking out across the street to see if he could proceed unseen. The pistol at her throat destroyed Sarah's desire to shout some sort of alarm to the men in the saloon and boarding house. Cantrell looked carefully all along the street, knowing that a careless move might expose him to the town defenders, although he counted on the thick darkness to mask him.

He bent down and talked darkly into Sarah's ear. "You move along in front of me, real slow, doing nothing to draw attention. If you so much as make a wrong step and expose us to anybody else, then I swear you'll take a bullet. That's an absolute guarantee. You understand?"

Sarah nodded quickly, and Cantrell gave a deathly, sickening sort of smile.

"Move on, then. Now."

The pair stepped out into the street, Cantrell holding Sarah closely, making it difficult for her to walk. As they progressed he half-carried, half-shoved her along, hugging close to the wall and staying in the shadows.

"We're going around toward the back of the Lodgepole. I don't want anyone to see us, not even my own men. You keep that in mind, you hear?"

He rounded the corner of the old livery and headed along the side of the adjacent building, cutting around the rear of the structure and toward the Lodgepole. Sarah could make out the dark form of a man on the rooftop, a rifle in his hands. But he appeared to be looking toward the main street, not noticing the pair that moved carefully along in the shadows.

Cantrell looked at the man, scowling, apparently fearful of moving further. But the man stood and headed forward, and for a moment there was no one within potential sight of Cantrell and Sarah.

Standing in the rear of the Lodgepole was a small storage building made of narrow logs joined together in the style of a stockade or French log house. There was a stout pine door on the structure, and it stood ajar. Cantrell shoved Sarah toward the building.

"Get inside." He pushed her forward, and she fell to her face in a sea of grime and greasy dirt. She looked back over her shoulder, trying to fight off tears.

Cantrell was digging in his pocket, and after a

moment produced a padlock. He dangled it on his finger at her, smiling. "I came prepared, you see!" Then the pine door slammed shut, the noise of the lock closing on the latch filtered through it, and Sarah was left alone in the darkness.

She heard Cantrell moving away, and through a space between two of the upright logs she saw him heading into the alley between the Lodgepole and the adjacent building. In moments he would be back inside the saloon, and no one would have any idea of what he had done. She was trapped.

She could cry for help, of course, but the only men close enough to hear her would be Cantrell's men—and Cantrell himself. She could make no escape attempt without him finding out about it, for the first thing any men who heard her would do would be to notify the man who was leading them—Rand Cantrell.

At least she was alive and unhurt, she told herself. But what of Kathy?

She was mystified by Kathy Denning's actions. Why the lady who before had stood so staunchly beside Rand Cantrell would make such a sudden change she couldn't be sure. Before Kathy had helped the gambler spread his lies; now she had risked her own life to keep him from hurting the very lady who had in a sense stolen the man she loved. To Sarah it was all very perplexing.

Sarah had been prepared to turn herself over to Noah Murphy, knowing full well it probably would result in her death. But she couldn't stand aside and watch the entire town being destroyed without doing something to stop it. She had tried, though unsuccessfully, thanks to Rand Cantrell.

Why did he need her? "A ticket out of town," he had said. The implications of that statement were not clear. Why would he need a hostage? It all implied that for some reason he would need protection when all of this

162

was over. There was something wrong going on, something secretive that made Sarah's skin crawl. She huddled back into the darkness, the cold gripping her, and she shivered in a numbed silence.

In the devastated saloon Charley had finished making his defense preparations. Rubble had been gathered and stacked in front of the building, and temporary props had been thrown up beneath the sagging portion of the upper floor. It was all very rickety and weak, and Charley knew that one well-placed bomb would blow it all away, but there was nothing more to be done.

The continued absence of the Murphy gang gave him more worry than comfort. He was smart enough to know that they weren't finished with the town, and probably intended to let the town sweat before renewing their attack. And Charley figured what happened then would be even worse than before.

He glanced toward the Lodgepole. Rand Cantrell was nowhere in sight, but then he hadn't been throughout the battle. At least his men had fought well, and all the previous stir over just who would give the orders seemed a bit pointless now. In the heat of the battle there had been little time to worry about such things, and at least Cantrell had stayed out of the way. Charley looked at the men seated above the roofline of the Lodgepole. Most were staring out into the darkness outside of town, waiting, just like everyone else. But he noticed one man—it looked like Joe Marcus—staring at him. When he returned the stare, Marcus looked quickly away. Charley lifted his eyebrows for a moment, then turned and immediately forgot the incident, seeing nothing of significance in it. But when his back was toward Joe Marcus, the young roughneck began staring at him again, a cold sort of glimmer in his eye.

Charley went over to the boarding house once more

to see how Doc was progressing. He found some of the wounded moved into the rear hallway, with Doc still probing for a bullet in one thin man who had taken a shot in his side. The old doctor was sweating and looking weary, and Charley knew better than to speak to him. He moved quickly past him and on to the rear room where the non-combatant residents of Dry Creek waited out the night.

He stepped over a cot holding a pale man who seemed to be hardly breathing, then entered the room and looked around.

"Where's Sarah?"

"She took out of here a while back. Kathy Denning went after her. Ain't seen either one of 'em since."

Charley frowned. "Did they say where they were goin'?"

"No. Didn't ask 'em."

Charley left the room. Sarah. . .leaving? Followed by Kathy? That worried him. And it wasn't like Sarah to disobey orders. But she had left the room in strict violation of what he had said. Sudden fear raced through his mind, and he felt a panicked desire to find Sarah Redding just as fast as he could.

Charley headed on out into the darkness that was broken only by the flickering light of the torches. A young man was replacing the torches that had burned out, and Charley grabbed his shoulder with such suddenness that the young man tensed.

"Do you know Sarah Redding?"

"Yes, sir."

"Have you seen her in the last few minutes?"

"No, sir—"

The boy was interrupted by a sudden explosion of shouting from the far end of the street. Men came running through the mixture of mud and snow that covered the wide expanse, and Charley knew even before they shouted the words that the attack had been resumed.

The figures on horseback bolted through the darkness more quickly than Charley would have thought possible, and no sooner had they reached the edge of the circle of faint light cast by the torches did they begin firing at the men who frantically tried to dart back behind the makeshift breastworks and barricades that were scattered in front of the devastated saloon and in the alleys. And by some miracle all of them made it, though the boy to whom Charley had been talking was clipped in the shoulder by a high-powered bullet.

Charley leaped headlong through the air to land in the alley between the saloon and boarding house. He had recovered his rifle from the street during the break in the fighting, and now he trained the sight on a figure astride one of the horses that were making graceful leaps across the barricade on the opposite end of the street where the fighting had scarcely touched. He squeezed the trigger; his eyes were blurred momentarily by a thick fog of gunsmoke, and through the white haze he saw the figure throw his arms to the sky and pitch backward into the snow.

Charley leaped up and headed for the saloon, but a bullet clipped at his heels and he dropped back to his previous position, looking wildly around.

The bullet had come unexpectedly from the opposite side of the street. Charley looked toward the gunsmithy, a building that before had been deserted. But the fading puff of smoke hanging in front of the window of the dark building was adequate proof that the place was deserted no more.

"Murphy gang has slipped in," Charley muttered to himself. He raised his rifle and blasted out a pane of glass, hoping his shot did some damage to the gunman inside.

But a rifle muzzle poked out through the broken pane and began spitting fire again, a twin muzzle shattering the adjoining window and doing the same. Charley ducked down, and then he heard the noise of the riders returning.

A dozen horses leaped the barricade and came tearing down the middle of the street. Charley fired a shot, missed, but was happy to see that some of the gunmen in the saloon beside him had better luck. Three riders pitched to the earth. One of them was trampled by the horses behind him, the others lay still as quickly as they struck the ground.

But the riders who made it managed to spit out a steady rain of bullets into the front of the saloon and along the roof of the Lodgepole. Charley saw one of Cantrell's men pitch forward to sprawl in the street, and the other men firing from the rooftop ducked downward to escape the hail of bullets.

Charley used the confusion of the moment to make his move toward the Mansfield Saloon. He ducked his head low and moved swiftly along the few feet of boardwalk between him and his goal. Bullets erupted from somewhere to splat into the wall beside him and into the boardwalk at his feet.

He threw himself over the breastworks at the front of the building and rolled as he struck to break his fall. He came up beside Bo Myers.

"Somebody about plugged me that time, Bo. Them Murphys. . ."

"It wasn't the Murphys, Charley. Those shots came from the Lodgepole. I saw 'em."

"What?"

"Somebody at the Lodgepole just shot at you!"

Charley was stunned. Hardly thinking about the danger of exposure, he lifted his head and peered over the rubble that protected the fighters.

A bullet struck inches from his face, stinging and hot. He ducked quickly down, and a shiver ran over him.

Bo was right. The shot had come from the Lodgepole. "I never would have thought Cantrell would go this far."

The man beside Charley—the marshal knew him only as a distant cousin of Kathy Denning—raised up and began moving toward the other side of the building. His grunt of pain came simultaneously with the roar of gunfire from the Lodgepole, and the man struck the floor dead.

Sudden anger overwhelmed the fighters in the Mansfield, and before Charley got halfway through realizing the bullet that had killed the man was meant for him, there was the sudden roar of fifteen rifles and the smell of burnt powder in the air.

The fighters in the Mansfield sent a fusillade of bullets toward the Lodgepole, and atop the log building the men who had declared their loyalty to Rand Cantrell threw themselves on their faces to keep from having their heads taken away by singing lead.

One of them wriggled his way over to Joe Marcus, who lay panting with a wild look in his eye, cursing himself to having missed Charley Hanna.

"What the hell are you tryin' to do? You fool—you've turned this into a three-way fight!" And before Joe could speak, a meaty hand came up and pounded hard into his face, splitting his lip and jarring him into a daze. He hardly knew what was happening when he felt rough hands grabbing him, lifting him up, then he was conscious of the mushy white and brown of the slush-covered street rushing up at him, and he struck the earth just as an explosion of bullets from across the street, fired in spite of protests by Charley Hanna, blasted away his life.

But the battle was on now, and it could not be

stopped. Men atop the Lodgepole sent answering blasts across the street, and Charley Hanna gave up hope of stopping the insane civil war between the townsfolk. Rand Cantrell's lies and bitterness had at last drawn blood—innocent, needlessly spilt blood.

Chapter 17

Noah Murphy stared incredulously from his position in the gunsmithy at the unexpected battle taking place between the townsfolk who before had been fighting what looked like a unified battle against him. But it was obvious that now they were shooting at each other as often as at his own men, and that astounded him.

He was bitter about the heavy toll the town had taken already on his men. He had led a large force against Dry Creek, and the town had already managed to cut it almost in half. Not that he worried too much about the loss of his men; the gang had been growing a bit too large for his comfort lately anyway, and he had suffered some secret doubts about how long he would be able to keep control over so large a group. Many of the men he had sent searching through the mountains for the money Willy had hidden had rejoined the main body of the gang before the attack, and Noah had anticipated no such battle as the one the town had given him.

But he was ready to move in for the kill now. With the town so inexplicably divided against itself the job might be made easier. And with his men now fired up with the desire for battle, they would be willing to take more risks than when their heads were more clear. Noah Murphy figured to lose several more gang members before this was over, but that was fine with him—just so he succeeded in putting Dry Creek through as much hell as possible without getting burned himself.

He heard the sound of his men's horses moving once more down the street, beginning what he hoped would be the climax of the fight. He gritted his teeth and stared with a glittering eye at the riders as they galloped past him, their forms bent low in the saddles and bombs flaring in their hands.

Charley Hanna watched the riders from his position at the front of the Mansfield Saloon, knowing full well what was coming. At the last fateful moment he fired his rifle at the lead rider, knocking him from the saddle just as he threw his handbomb deep into the saloon. The other riders followed suit, and a moment before the saloon was again rendered with blasts Charley was conscious of Bo's sudden movement—a kind of lunging action—and the cries of the men around him as they anticipated what was to come.

The explosions ripped through the saloon with devastating force, knocking what remained of the front wall out into the street, crumbling the walls on either side, flipping bodies about like dust in the prairie wind. Charley felt his body being lifted from the floor by the concussion of one of the bottles exploding near him, then something heavy collapsed on top of him and for a moment there was only darkness.

Then a pinpoint of light reached him, and he stared in numbed confusion at it. His reeling brain realized that he was looking through a gap in the rubble that had fallen on top of him, seeing the street in front of the building.

Horses and riders lay about, as if kicked aside by some force that had exploded in the midst of them.

Charley recalled the movement Bo had made just before the blasts came, and he heard himself laughing. Bo had thrown his last bomb, right into the midst of the riders, just as they had thrown their powder-filled bottles into the saloon. And the blast had taken a hard toll on Murphy's gang.

Charley was choked with dust, and from the sharp pain in his thigh he felt as if something sharp had stabbed him. He twisted his head—it hurt to do it—and saw that a nail had dug into his thigh after being ripped from the beam in which it had been imbedded. The weight crushing into Charley was almost unbearable, and he realized that the ceiling had collapsed.

He looked out through the opening into the street again, seeing one of the Murphy riders rising from where he had been knocked to the ground by the blast. The man appeared stunned and hardly able to control his movements, for he staggered and almost fell as quickly as he made it to his feet. As Charley watched there was the sound of one of the fighters at the Lodgepole firing his rifle, and the man jerked and fell to the earth. More shots came then, fired at the other downed Murphy riders, and Charley knew that in moments all of them would be massacred by Cantrell's gunmen.

And the threat of the Murphys would virtually be over. Only two or three gunmen—those who had secreted themselves in the gunsmith's shop—would remain. But now that Cantrell's men had so treacherously turned on the townsfolk, Charley wasn't sure whether the situation would be any better.

But before he could do anything at all he would have to free himself from the rubble that held him trapped. He looked around him as much as his cramped situation would allow. He heard moans from other men around him, and the sound of feet scrambling somewhere to his left. Then the rubble around him moved, and he twisted his head to see Martin Arlo pulling the ragged beams

171

and timber away from him. The nail in his thigh pulled free, racking him for a moment with even more intense pain.

"Charley, I'll have you outta here before. . ."

Martin Arlo jerked simultaneously with the sound of the shot, and he pitched forward. Warm blood dripped onto Charley's face, and he felt suddenly weak.

He pushed Arlo's form up from him and raised himself up, trying to see if all his extremities still moved normally. Arlo groaned as Charley rolled him aside and went for his pistol. He drew and fired one shot at the rifleman atop the Lodgepole, and the rifle went flying as the man pitched backward from the force of the .44 shell striking his chest.

Charley crawled out atop the rubble, dragging the wounded Arlo by the shoulders to the rear of the heap of fallen ceiling timbers. Shots rained into the saloon, fired by Lodgepole gunmen, and Charley felt the flesh of his shoulder rip as a shell winged past him, taking some of his skin with it. He dropped to the grit-covered floor behind Arlo, then raised up to fire another shot at the shoulders and heads that bobbed up on top of the Lodgepole long enough to aim and fire.

He heard shooting coming from the boarding house, and realized that the few gunmen who had been stationed there were giving a tough fight to the Lodgepole gunmen. Staccato rifle blasts came from farther up the street, and Charley guessed that the Murphy gunmen in the gunsmith shop were making it hot for the boarding house fighters.

And that in turn would be endangering the wounded men that Doc was tending in the boarding house lobby. Charley saw several of the men in the saloon pull themselves from under the collapsed ceiling and dust off their weapons. Though clearly the blasts and subsequent devastation in the building had killed several men, many

172

others were merely wounded and ready to fight again. He set his mouth in a line of grim satisfaction as the battle swelled again, more rifles and handguns adding their roar to the noise of fighting.

Charley thought fleetingly of Sarah. It plagued him to wonder where she was, especially now that the fighting was so fierce. He breathed a silent prayer for her safety. He felt a sudden shame when he realized that Kathy too was gone and perhaps in as great a danger as Sarah, and he whispered another quick prayer for Kathy to ease his conscience.

From the looks of things not one of the Murphy riders who had so recently bolted down the street had managed to escape alive. The battle was primarily between the people of Dry Creek now, though there was still the group in the gunsmithy to think about.

Charley noted that the saloon now had several fighters in the battle, enough to keep a steady rain of fire on the Lodgepole. A plan began formulating in his mind, and he looked down at Martin Arlo.

The man was pale and clearly in pain, but the wound in his shoulder didn't look too severe. Charley leaned down close to talk to him.

"Martin—you gonna be all right here? I can't get you to the Doc with this fighting goin' so hard."

"I'll be all right. I reckon I won't die, Charley."

Charley stared at Arlo for a moment, then he was gone, moving out the back door of the saloon and heading along the back of the row of buildings and in the direction of the church house.

He kept a close eye on the forests to his left as he moved, for he feared there might be more Murphy fighters left than he guessed. But there was no sign of movement from the dark treeline, and he traveled swiftly and without difficulty.

He passed the shattered hut in which Bo had cast his

first bomb. In the dimness of the ruptured building he could see the blast-contorted bodies of the men who had died there. Bo had done an efficient job. Charley realized suddenly that the deputy had been beside him when the ceiling collapsed, and that he had not emerged from the rubble to rejoin the fight. Was he dead? Charley hoped not, but he realized it was a good possibility.

Charley used the buildings and alley barricades for cover as he moved. When he reached the snowy yard between the final building on the street and the church house which sat back from it several yards, he stopped long enought to empty the spent shells from his pistol cylinder and replace them with live ammunition.

He slipped the pistol back into his holster as he rounded the rear of the building, staying close to the wall and moving as silently as he could. The silence really wasn't necessary—the noise of fighting would likely cover any noise he might make—but he wanted to be careful, so he moved cat-like in a tense stalking position around the side of the building.

The barricade stretched out before him, completely undamaged from any of the fighting, for all of the battle had so far been concentrated on the far end of the street. Charley reached the corner of the building where the barricade began, then he dropped to his knees in the snow and peered over the top of the breastworks.

The gunsmith shop was across the street and down about a hundred feet in the row of buildings. As Charley had suspected, the Murphy fighters still were there, for he could see the muzzles of their weapons protruding from the windows as they fought.

He dropped to his belly and began wriggling forward in the snow. The snow chilled his skin and soaked his clothing as it melted against the heat of his body, but he proceeded with determination, keeping himself low and out of view of the street.

It took him longer than he had anticipated to make it across the wide street, and when at last he crawled to safety on the side of the building there he was winded from the exertion of the unnatural means of travel.

He stood up, brushing the snow from his pants, and moved toward the rear of the building. Once there, he drew his pistol and steeled his nerve.

It had appeared that only two gunmen were in the gunsmithy, but he couldn't be sure just yet. What he was about to do might accomplish nothing more than getting him killed. But then it just might also accomplish the final defeat of the Murphys. That is, if he could preserve the element of surprise until the last moment.

He stepped forward, his boot crunching a little too loudly in the snow and making him wince. But there was no response to the noise, so after a moment's pause he continued.

From this angle there was no visible sign of battle. Only the noise of gunshots gave evidence of the fight. Here in the safety of the backside of the main street buildings things appeared totally peaceful, and the incongruity of it all grated on Charley's nerves as he thought of what would come next.

He moved further down the row until he reached the gunsmith shop. The rear door stood ajar, and inside Charley could hear the sound of the two men moving around and talking, along with the occasional sound of gunfire.

A voice reached him from the interior.

"Noah, I think we should get out of here."

"Shut up. They blasted away my whole damn gang, and I'll make 'em pay as best I can for that. Get to shootin'!"

"Noah, it's just a matter of time before they get to us,

'less we ran right now.''

"I said shut up!"

Charley twisted his lips, whistling silently in surprise. Noah Murphy himself was in there, it seemed. The gang leader himself, the man responsible for all of this. Charley felt a sudden morbid happiness surge through him; what came next would give him quite a sense of satisfaction if it worked out well.

He checked his pistol, then stepped forward as carefully as he could. His form moved to the open doorway, and he squinted as he peered inside.

The door opened onto the rear room of the building, from which another doorway led into the front room where Noah Murphy and his companion were. Charley's lips tightened into a smile as he carefully stepped inside, and his heart pounded loudly. The feeling coursing through him was a strange one—kind of a fearful elation—but it steeled his nerve and gave him a strong determination to do what might not be easy to accomplish.

Pausing to prepare himself, he moved forward another step. Just as his foot touched the floor there was a sudden, unexpected break in the fighting, and in the moment of silence the sound of his footfall carried through the open doorway into the front room.

"What was that?" Noah Murphy's companion voiced the question.

Charley moved forward, literally leaping through the doorway, cocking back the hammer of his .44 at the same time. Noah Murphy's face went suddenly pale, and his partner cried out as if stung by a hornet.

"Nobody but me," said Charley as he squeezed down on the trigger of his pistol.

The roar reverberated through the tiny room, shaking the walls and deafening Charley to the sound of the grunting noise Murphy's partner made as three slugs ripped through him. As he fell Noah Murphy tossed aside his empty rifle with a roar of rage, and his hand dropped swiftly to his sidearm.

Not swiftly enough. Charley turned the .44 Colt on the outlaw, gritting his teeth and emptying the gun into the man's chest and stomach. Murphy thrashed and jerked as the lead struck him, then he collapsed to his knees, holding his arms across his torso and staring with a look of agonized anger at the man he knew had killed him.

Charley stared without pity at the man through the cloud of gunsmoke. "Sorry I had to do that, cousin," he said.

Noah Murphy's eyes glazed and he fell stiffly forward, his body making a thudding noise as he struck the floor. Charley looked down at him and slipped his gun back into his holster.

The feeling that had gripped him throughout the last minutes left him, and suddenly he felt ill. Lurching out through the back door of the building, he began to vomit.

Chapter 18

Kathy Denning struggled to her feet in the dark, deserted livery stable. She was dizzy, cold, and disoriented, and for a long time she stood in confusion, trying to determine her whereabouts and what was causing the roaring, blasting noises from outside. Then as her mind cleared she recalled what had happened, and realized that the noise was that of battle. The Murphys apparently had resumed their attack.

She felt suddenly fearful and looked around her. But none of the outlaw gang's members were present, it seemed, and she relaxed somewhat. She moved to the open doorway of the livery, taking care to conceal herself, and looked out into the street.

The saloon was devastated, much of the wall gone and the ceiling collapsed. And the bodies strewn in the street seemed to be those of Murphy's gang. And all appeared dead.

Yet the battle was continuing, for the gunfire was as heavy as before. Kathy was confused. If the Murphy gang was wiped out, as it appeared, then who could be fighting?

She moved back into the darkness of the livery, awed and somehow angry. Apparently Rand Cantrell's dividing of the town had reached the ultimate, breaking into open battle. Kathy felt guilt stir in her as she thought of how the lies she had spread for Cantrell had added to the division of the town. But she never could have imagined it would come to this.

Cantrell could not be allowed to get away with this. He had to be stopped. He had taken Sarah Redding as a hostage to insure his safe escape from Dry Creek, so Kathy knew that any move to stop him would have to happen soon or he would be gone into the mountains. Once he escaped the confines of the town it would be unlikely that he would ever be found again.

She stepped back into the door of the livery and waited until the confusion of battle made it unlikely she would be seen. Then she stepped quickly around the corner of the door and headed into the alley.

She heard the noise of a man crying out on top of the Lodgepole as she neared the building, and a heavy body fell to the ground just inches from where she stood. She gasped and stepped back, pressing her hand to her heart. Then she noticed the .44 Colt still gripped in the man's hand, and she knelt down to pick it out of his grasp.

Across the street in the saloon Bo Myers had at last managed to crawl out from under the heavy beam that had held him pinned to the floor. He rubbed his head, wincing, feeling the large, raw knot there. His gun was lost somewhere under the rubble, but there were plenty of loose weapons about, dropped by wounded men or held in the cold hands of dead ones. He picked up a half-loaded Henry from the floor and tried to focus his eyes enough to join in the fighting.

He took aim at a figure on top of the log building across the street. The man in his sights was just drawing a bead on one of the men in the Mansfield Saloon when Bo fired. The young deputy was honestly surprised when his shot struck the man, for he had been very uncertain and wavering in his aim. He levered a new cartridge into the rifle chamber and waited for another target to appear.

He noticed the rifle muzzle probing out of the small

window on the west end of the Lodgepole, and he squinted into the darkness of the window to try to make out who was firing the rifle. He thought that the shadowy face that was faintly visible looked like that of Rand Cantrell, but he wasn't certain. He hadn't laid eyes on Cantrell since the beginning of the fight. It seemed the gambler was making himself as scarce as possible.

Bo raised his rifle and aimed carefully at the small window. When he saw the faint white movement of the man behind it again, he fired, then lowered his weapon to stare into the small dark square.

No movement for a long time. Bo grinned. If that had been Cantrell in there it wasn't likely he would cut another deck of cards ever again.

But hardly had Bo become convinced he had killed Cantrell when suddenly the rifle muzzle poked out again, firing more steadily this time, as if the man at the trigger was angry. Bo ducked down and cursed at himself. It seemed his shooting wasn't as good as he had thought.

As the battle progressed he looked at the situation. With the men in and on the Lodgepole so well covered the odds were that the fight would continue for hours without any substantial losses to Cantrell's side. Compared to the stance of Cantrell's gunmen, the men in the Mansfield Saloon were in a much poorer situation. Though there was plenty of rubble in which to hide, Cantrell's men had a clearer field of fire and could afford to aim more carefully as they fought, while the men in the Mansfield could scarcely get off an effective shot at their enemies without exposing themselves dangerously for long, tense moments. If the men in the Lodgepole had plenty of ammunition, their fewer numbers would be no disadvantage. They could afford to wait out the fight, aiming carefully until they had wiped out the enemy.

Bo fired a few more shots, but after a time he became discouraged. The fight wouldn't be won like this. He knew that only because of his timely tossing of the bomb had the Murphys been defeated. It would take a similar move to bring down the Cantrell men.

But what could he do? He had tossed his last bomb, and he couldn't get another.

Just as the thought crossed his mind he saw it—another bomb laying half-buried in the slushy snow just outside the ruptured front of the saloon. It had apparently been the dampness of the ground that caused the fuse to fizzle out before reaching the powder. But it was a bomb—one that would work if only Bo could get to it.

But how? Bo looked at the bomb, longing for the feel of it in his hand, thinking of the satisfaction it would give him to hear it rending the roof of the Lodgepole into splinters after a well-aimed throw.

It almost made his mouth water to think about it. If only he could get to it, break off the moist and useless portion of the fuse, get a match to the remainder. . .He shook off the idea. It would take too long and be far too dangerous to attempt it. A man could get himself killed.

That thought raced over and over through Bo's mind as he forced himself up over the heap of rubble and toward the bottle. He didn't look around him nor pay attention to the burst of gunfire that intensified suddenly from the Lodgepole. His only goal was to get his hands around that bottle, to have it safely in his grasp while he darted back toward the Mansfield.

His leg collapsed beneath him, suddenly numb, and blood ran down his pants leg. He pushed himself back up and continued forward, his hand groping outward for the bottle.

A bullet ripped through his left shoulder, sending a

shiver of pain through his side and making him shudder. But even as he pitched himself forward and felt his fingers close around the coldness of the bottle he knew he wouldn't give up on what he was doing until he was either dead or watching the Lodgepole roof crumbling to splinters.

He rolled to one side and broke the water-soaked fuse off near the top of the bottle all in one motion. Rifle slugs tore up the earth inches from him. Had he not rolled he would have been killed instantly.

His good hand gripped the bottle, and he forced his wounded arm to move just enough to allow him to dig for the box of matches in his pocket. He found it and pulled it out, wincing with pain. Another bullet ripped through his foot, and he tried to not faint from the pain.

He dropped the bottle to the crook of his elbow and held it there as he rolled once more. Again the maneuver saved him and lead plowed the earth perilously close to him. But in the midst of it all he managed to get a match lit, and some incredible reserve of strength suddenly gave him the power to rise as he touched the flaring match head to the short fuse.

He grasped the bottle in his right hand, raising it high above his head. He wished he could toss the bomb through the small window where Cantrell was hidden, but he knew he couldn't afford to risk missing the small opening and rendering his sacrifice useless.

And a tremendous sacrifice it was. Bo didn't doubt that he was living out his final moments of life. Into his mind flashed the night that he had in a sense started it all by telling Rand Cantrell the contorted story about Charley Hanna's knowledge of the hidden Murphy money, and for a moment, just as he tossed the bottle, he was grimly satisfied that what he was doing now would make it right again, even out the score.

Bo didn't hear the rending blast of the bottle, for his

life had been blown away by the hot lead of Rand Cantrell's rifle a moment before the bottle exploded. But the gambler had no chance to bask in the delight of his kill, for the ceiling above him suddenly was shattered, splinters, dirt, and metal spikes filled the air, and the cries of the men blown off the rooftop by the blast or dropped into the interior of the log building mixed with the deafening sound of cracking, falling timbers. Cantrell cried out and threw his hands above his head in a futile attempt to protect himself.

In the darkness of the small shed behind the Lodgepole, Sarah Redding heard the blast and sound of the crashing timbers. She jumped, startled, and wondered what had happened. She assumed the Murphy gang must have managed to destroy the Lodgepole. Mixed emotions came to her; she had no desire to be the victim of Noah Murphy and his men, but then she felt being the prisoner of Rand Cantrell would hardly be better.

Her only hope lay in Charley Hanna's ability to overcome both Murphy and Cantrell, and that seemed too big a demand even for a man of his strength and courage. She shivered in the darkness, fighting despair.

After a time it became unbearable to remain still, and she stood and began moving around the small hut. Light issued in diffusely through the small cracks between the upright logs, and she moved over to the widest opening and peered through, trying to see something of what was happening at the Lodgepole.

She could make out dust and smoke issuing from the roof of the building, though the walls were apparently undamaged. No men were atop the flat structure, and she assumed that the roof had collapsed in the blast she had heard moments before.

She found herself hoping that Rand Cantrell had died under the crushing weight of the roof. She wasn't a lady accustomed to wishing injury or death to anyone, but never before had she encountered anyone so worthy of hate as Rand Cantrell. Even Noah Murphy didn't seem like such a devil as Cantrell, for he at least was openly and unapologetically evil, while Cantrell hid his diabolical nature beneath a veneer of smoothness and deception. So capable was he of presenting himself as righteous and altruistic that he at one point had convinced the majority of Dry Creek's normally sensible folks that he should be followed. That seemed incredible to Sarah now, even more than it had before.

She couldn't see much through the small opening, but the sound of continuing gunfire let her know that the fight wasn't yet over. The sound of shooting intensified, then declined suddenly.

Sarah was concious of a shadowy movement across the crack through which she was peering, and the padlock rattled suddenly on the door. Sarah gasped and moved to the far wall of the structure, her breath coming fast and hard.

The door swung open to reveal Rand Cantrell, disheveled and dirty. He gripped a pistol in his left hand. His right was torn and bleeding and hung limply at his side.

"Move!" he hissed, no longer attempting to retain his usual air of calm and placidness. "Get out of here, and don't make a sound."

Sarah obeyed, trembling. Cantrell moved his wounded hand out and grabbed her weakly, leveling the pistol on her temple.

"I got two horses over here, hid out," he said. "Go get on the mare. And if you do anything at all to make your presence known I'll kill you!"

Cantrell had the air of a desperate man. His hurried actions and worried expression told her he had no time to spare. He glanced over his shoulder at the alleyway beside the Lodgepole. As he grasped Sarah's arm his hand was trembling.

He shoved her forward. She stumbled but managed to keep her balance. Cantrell glanced nervously over his shoulder once more, shoving her again.

"Where are we going from here?" she said.

"You'll find out soon enough."

"The pass is blocked. And we'll never survive long in the mountains."

"Shut up and move."

A man appeared in the alleyway. He raised his pistol and prepared to fire at Cantrell, but the gambler shoved Sarah between him and the man, stopping him from shooting. Cantrell's pistol came up and fired, and the man fell back against the wall, gripping a wounded forearm. Before Cantrell could send a fatal shot into him, he backed off into the safety of the alley.

Cantrell pushed Sarah forward to where two horses, already saddled and shivering from being exposed for hours to the cold, stood waiting in a hidden clearing in a stand of spruce. Sarah mounted the gray mare that Cantrell pointed her toward, and the gambler mounted a tan gelding, grunting with pain as he climbed up. He had a long gash in his arm, apparently an injury suffered when the roof of the Lodgepole collapsed.

He clicked his tongue and gouged his heels into the flanks of his horse and began moving forward.

No sooner had they moved out of the hidden clearing into the open area directly in back of the southern row of buildings on Dry Creek's main street than a female voice, quivering yet threatening, called out, "Stop, Cantrell. Stop or I'll shoot you."

The gambler jerked and turned his head. Sarah looked in the direction from which the voice had come, and stared into the pale and frightened face of Kathy Denning, who stood gripping a .44 with both hands.

The muzzle of the fearsome weapon was aimed at Rand Cantrell's chest.

Cantrell glared at the woman for a moment, then his face calmed, and the same deceptive, smooth air that usually hung about him returned. He smiled at Kathy. "Kathy, what are you doing? You know you couldn't pull that trigger."

"I could, Rand. And I will if you move."

Cantrell sat slumping in his saddle, studying Kathy. Then his hand whipped to his side and drew out the pistol that hung there. But instead of leveling it on Kathy he aimed the muzzle at Sarah, clicking back the hammer and holding it with his thumb while his finger squeezed the trigger.

"Shoot, then. But you know as soon as my finger lets up on this trigger Mrs. Redding here will be gone. Do you want that?"

Kathy looked at the gambler, a mixture of loathing and sorrow on her face. Slowly she lowered the pistol, then let it drop to her side. Cantrell smiled.

"Thank you, Kathy Denning. Now we'll be bothered with you no more." He swung up his pistol and fired a shot at the woman. She cried out, her feet kicking out from under her as the force of the bullet knocked her down. Sarah screamed as Kathy fell, and Rand Cantrell laughed.

His laugh stopped suddenly when he turned to look squarely into the muzzle of Charley Hanna's pistol. The marshal approached in the dim light of the diminishing darkness. The sun cast a faint, feeble ray over the eastern horizon, and it glimmered on the muzzle of Charley's pistol. And when Rand Cantrell gave his calm smile it flashed also on his straight white teeth.

"Hello, Marshal. Looks like you caught me." The gambler's finger moved almost imperceptibly on the trigger of his pistol. Charley noticed the movement.

"I wouldn't, Rand. I'll blow you out of that saddle."

"Now, Marshal, you don't think I would be such a fool as to. . ." The gambler dropped suddenly from his saddle, lunging for Sarah as he fell, cocking back the hammer of his pistol. He dragged her from her saddle, landing nimbly on his feet with an agility that took Charley by surprise. He jammed the gun up into her throat, grinning in triumph at the marshal.

"Drop the gun or I'll kill her," he snarled. "Now!"

Charley's eyes were cold as he stared at Rand Cantrell. He did not break his gaze from the gambler's eyes as he raised his pistol. Cantrell's smile wavered, then faded, and he pushed the barrel of his pistol hard into Sarah's throat.

"I swear I'll kill her. . .I swear it!"

Charley fired one shot. It was sufficient. Cantrell took the bullet in the forehead, and he was dead before his body struck the ground. Sarah stood horribly transfixed for a moment, then cried out and rushed toward Charley, throwing her arms around him. Charley Hanna put one arm around her, and let the other drop to his side, the pistol dangling in his hand. He stared straight at the body of Rand Cantrell, his face blank and stony.

Chapter 19

Kathy Denning wasn't as severely wounded as the doc first thought. He took the bullet from her shoulder and confined her to her bed. Sarah Redding entered the room shortly after Kathy was put to bed, and the two of them talked for a long time by themselves. When Sarah emerged she appeared happy, but she refused to reveal just what had been discussed.

Charley could figure it out anyway. He had only just realized that—incredible though it was—Kathy had been in love with him for months. He couldn't imagine how he could have never noticed before.

But once he realized that he understood a little better why she had done what she did. It had been intense, irrational jealousy that had led her to Rand Cantrell and moved her to participate in spreading lies about him. But she had more than made up for her error in the brave way she had challenged the gambler in the predawn darkness.

Dry Creek was a devastated, miserable town, if such a word could even describe the pitiful remnant of the population that remained. The death count was a horrible affair, and the figure mounted so rapidly that Charley refused to hear the final tally. There was no time for individual funerals—even for any decent embalming—so there was a mass funeral held under the direction of Preacher Bartlett, and all the townsfolk were buried in long rows of graves on the hillside. The outlaw gang and Rand Cantrell were buried in unmarked tombs in the forest, along with the men who had fought alongside the gambler. The survivors among Cantrell's men were locked away in the jailhouse. There were no surviving members of the Murphy gang.

Charley managed to piece together the full story from reports of men who had fought in the Mansfield Saloon. When Bo Myers had sacrificed his own life in order to deal the death-stroke to the Lodgepole Saloon, Rand Cantrell had been trapped beneath the roof timbers along with most of the other Lodgepole occupants. But the gambler had fought desperately when the men from the Mansfield moved across the street to make good the capture, and he had managed to escape, in the process severely wounding three men. It was then that he had taken Sarah from her tiny prison and made his ill-fated escape attempt.

Martin Arlo recovered well from his wounds as the days passed, and Charley made him an official full-time deputy. The marshal's face reflected the intense sadness that the loss of Bo Myers brought him, for he had been close to his deputy, as scraggly, ill-mannered, and unkempt as he had been.

Doc Hopkins saw Charley and Sarah standing together in the graveyard on an unseasonably warm evening about three weeks after what had generally come to be known as "Dry Creek's bad night." The old sawbones shuffled up the hillside to where the couple stood overlooking the graves of Martha Hanna and Bo Myers. Charley had insisted that Bo be buried not far from his mother as an honor to the brave deputy.

"Howdy, Doc. Good to see you."

"I reckon."

Sarah smiled. "I'm glad you came, Doc. We were

going to come looking for you in a few minutes anyway.''

Doc lifted his eyebrows. "Why is that?"

"We're leavin' tomorrow, Doc," Charley said. "We've talked about it, and we're ready to head for Denver to get married."

Doc smiled. "I'm not surprised. When will you be back?"

Charley glanced at Sarah. "We won't be back, Doc. We're leavin' for good."

The old man's face looked suddenly weary, and his eyes moistened noticeably. But he smiled at the couple, though sadly. "I reckon I don't blame you, Charley. If I wasn't so blasted old I think I would leave myself."

The old man looked down on the windswept, drab town of Dry Creek. The place was shabby, weatherbeaten. Everywhere there was slush and melting ice as the weather broke through the grip of winter in a temporary respite.

"The town is dead, Charley. At least it's dying. It won't ever be the same again, not after what's happened here. In a few years not many folks will ever know there was a Dry Creek. Noah Murphy and Rand Cantrell killed this town—and it took them with it."

"We don't want it spread that we're leaving, Doc," Charley said. "I told Martin Arlo to take over my duties. He'll be a good lawman. Ain't nobody gonna see us off but Kathy. . .and you, I hope."

Doc smiled. "I'll be there."

"I'm glad, Doc. And we want you to come and see us in Denver real soon," Sarah said. "Will you do that?"

The old man laughed. "I reckon I could. There's still a little wanderlust left in these old bones. But right now I could use a good cup of coffee"—he looked slyly around, then winked—"or maybe somethin' a little stronger. What d'you say?"

"I say that sounds like the best suggestion I've heard all day!" Charley said. "Lead the way, Doc."

The trio moved off, leaving the graveyard to be enshrouded in darkness. The only sound was the wild moaning of the wind in the mountains and the steady dripping of a melting icicle above the grave of Martha Hanna. Below in the town, Doc Hopkins pulled shut his office door and closed out the darkness, and night fell on Dry Creek.